HIS DECEPTION

HIS CONFESSION TRILOGY
BOOK 2

ANGEL RAYNE

ALSO BY ANGEL RAYNE

Mafia Romance Reading Order

Luca and Veda

His Game

His Stakes

His Win

Enzo and Sera

His Promise

His Rejection

His Proposal

Tristan and Luna

His Darkness

His Deception

His Destiny

Stand Alone Novels

Tyler and Ailee

Be With Me

SYNOPSIS

A monster made me a captive in the dark. Now, I'm starting to love it...and him...

When I first met Tristan, I thought he was cold. Heartless. Maybe even a sociopath.

I was right.

He stalked me. Kidnapped me. And now I'm his prisoner.

I want to hate him. I should hate him.

But I can't.

Not when he rescued me from an even bigger monster. Not when he's risked everything to protect me.

Not when he looks at me like I'm the only light he's ever had in his dark, tortured life.

I know I must do whatever is necessary to escape this cell. To survive.

I can only hope I have the strength to leave my monster
when the time comes...

CHAPTER 1

Tristan

I stared at the photo in my hands like I was seeing a ghost from another time. A more uncertain time. A different life than the one I led now. Because that's exactly what it was.

The woman in the photo was Luna, but not. If I looked closely, there were a few small differences. Luna's hair was the same shade—such a dark brown it was nearly black—but it was longer and thicker. Her lips were fuller. The shape of her face more heart-shaped than oval. She was also about fifteen to twenty pounds heavier, with larger breasts, curvier hips, and a rounder ass. Her skin was also a slightly different shade. Paler, creamier, without the olive tones of her Italian father.

The biggest difference between the two of them was that the woman I was staring at in the picture was cold and rotting in the ground and had been for the last seventeen years. Because I was the one who'd killed her.

But the hot-blooded woman in the back bedroom of my house, she was very much alive and well.

I closed my eyes. I could still feel the phantom weight of her warm, soft body pressed against my chest as I'd carried her unconscious form away from Gino's. Her head had lolled against my shoulder, her long dark hair spilling over my arm like ink. It had triggered memories I'd long ago tried to bury, a chilling reminder of the horrific nights that still haunted my dreams. No matter how hard I tried, I could never completely forget the things they'd done to me. Some sins could never be forgiven or forgotten.

And yet, even with my demons diving at me from every direction, I'd pulled her closer, my only desire to protect her from the haunting echoes of my long-ago trauma reaching her.

"Tristan."

Dragging my attention from the photo in my hand, I met Enzo's eyes. Or at least the approximate location of them behind the dark glasses he wore.

To my surprise, he took them off and set them on the table. We were sitting in my kitchen after he'd texted me that he was coming over. He didn't know I had Luna locked away in my cell, and unless he walked back there, he never would. Because that room was indeed completely soundproof, just as I'd told her when I'd gotten Enzo's text. She could be back there screaming her lungs out and neither of us would ever know.

Enzo caught my eyes with his, and I had to fight the urge to look away. Staring into Enzo's eyes was like being swept up by a tornado of emotions, complete with flashes of intense feelings he couldn't seem to control and hits from random pieces of judgmental debris. It was why he wore the glasses. His eyes gave everything away. I wished he'd put them back on. Having a conversation like this left me feeling unsettled for hours afterward, and so it took me a moment to realize he'd asked me a question. "I'm sorry?"

"I asked you if what you told Luca was true. About the woman Gino brought to my wedding."

I laid the picture face up on the table between us. "Yes, it's true."

"So, that's her mother. His wife that died."

"The woman I killed under Luigi's orders," I corrected. "Yes."

"Luca told me you're planning to take her from Gino."

I weighed my options. I could tell Enzo she was already here, or I could leave him in the dark and make my life more difficult than it had to be by hiding the fact from both Luca *and* Enzo that she was locked in my cell. Gino was bound to come looking for her, sooner rather than later, and it would be helpful if Enzo was aware of the situation so he could back up whatever story I chose to tell. "I already did. She's no longer residing with her father."

Enzo sat back in his chair. "You took her?"

"Yes."

"Where is she?"

"Here." I glanced toward the back of the house.

He followed my gaze. He knew what was back there. His eyes met mine again. "Did she come willingly?"

"I didn't give her a choice. So, no."

I watched the myriad of emotions tangle up within his eyes right before he shoved back his chair and stood. I didn't try to stop him as he strode from the kitchen and headed toward the back of the house. I knew it would be useless.

Sipping the glass of iced tea I'd poured for myself right after he'd gotten here, I listened as he opened the last door. Luna's pleading voice echoed down the hallway as she begged him to release her. Then the door closed again, and I heard him striding back to the kitchen. Rising slightly out of my chair, I reached across the table and refilled his glass with the bottle of whiskey I kept here for him and Luca. I never touched the stuff myself. Alcohol dulled your senses and made you lose control, and I didn't like it when I lost control.

A few seconds later, he sat back down across from me and swallowed the entire thing. "You have a woman locked in your cell."

It wasn't a question, but I confirmed it anyway. "Yes."

He was silent for a moment as he poured himself another drink. "Luca told me of your suspicions about Gino. So, I can only assume this is your fucked-up way of removing her from a dangerous situation."

This time, I didn't answer. There was no need. The reasons didn't really matter at this point, did they? She was here.

"Tristan, you can't keep her locked up in there."

"Yes, I can."

"Okay. Fair enough. You can. But you shouldn't."

I shrugged. Societal rules had never meant much to me. "I couldn't leave her there, Enzo."

He searched my face, but this time, my stare didn't falter. Although he knew how I was raised, there were things that happened during my upbringing he didn't know about. Things I would never tell him.

Finally, he sighed heavily. "What do you plan to do with her?"

"She's safe in there. No one, including her fucking rapist father, will be able to get to her, even if I'm not here. Unless he plans to try to shoot her again." I stared down at the cold glass between my hands and frowned. The odds were good Gino would do exactly that. To remove the temptation she represented and to keep her mouth shut.

"He tried to shoot her? How do you know that?"

"She told me."

Enzo scrubbed his face with his hand. "Why would he try to kill his own daughter?"

"Because he was fucking her. Using her as a replacement for the wife he lost." I spun the half-filled glass around with my fingers, watching the ice clink together.

"And you're absolutely positive that he was having sex with her?"

I swallowed down the bile that rose in my throat and shifted uncomfortably in my chair. "I saw it with my own eyes the first night I went to his house to see her. Before I knew who she was to him."

"Wait." He held up his hand. "You were in the house?"

"No. Outside. Watching through the window."

Disbelief crossed his face. "How many times have you done that?"

I shrugged one shoulder. It wasn't important. What mattered was that I'd seen what I had, and Luna had no idea she was playing the whore for her own fucking flesh and blood.

Enzo scrubbed a palm over his jaw, staring down at the black tabletop like it held the answers to all of life's questions. When he realized he wasn't going to find them there, he sighed again. This time with resignation. "I take it Luca doesn't know she's here."

I picked up the glass and swirled the tea around before taking a drink. I was bored with this conversation. I wanted to check on Luna. "No," I told him, setting the glass back on the table a bit harder than necessary. "He gave me a direct order to leave her with Gino."

"Which you ignored."

I raised an eyebrow in question. "Yes. We've established that. What's your point, Enzo?"

He gave a small shake of his head. "Sorry, T. I'm just trying to figure out what the hell is going on with you."

I met his eyes and let a tiny sliver of vulnerability show through. "I can't answer that question." Because I didn't know either. I didn't know why this woman was so fascinating to me. Or why I gave a shit about what happened to her. I only knew that she was. And I did. To the point that I was completely distracted when I wasn't near her and all I could think about was rushing back to her side. "I'm not going to hurt her, if that's what you're worried about."

He didn't try to deny it, and that was something I appreciated about both him and Luca. They always gave it to me straight. And knowing what they knew about me, it was a legitimate fear.

"What is it that you feel for this woman, T?"

"Feel?" I felt nothing. And everything.

"Yeah. Do you wanna fuck her? Brush her hair and dress her up like a doll? Or just keep her in that cage like some kind of sacrificial bird and make her sing for you?"

"I told you, I'm not going to hurt her."

"That doesn't answer my question."

"Because it's none of your fucking business."

"It is when you're about to cause a war within the family."

"I'll handle Gino. I'm just waiting for Luca to give me the go ahead."

He scoffed. "Why bother? Apparently, you just do whatever the hell you want to anyway."

"I wouldn't endanger Luca. Or you. And you damn well know it."

"What did you think would happen when you brought her here?" He pointed toward the room at the end of the hall. "Do you think Gino isn't going to come straight here looking for her? Demanding we return her to him?"

"He doesn't know it was me who took her. She was running from him when I caught up to her. He probably thinks she managed to get away. Besides, I don't give a shit what he demands. She's not going back there." I stood, feeling restless with this turn in our conversation. My mind spun with everything he said, but I wouldn't give Luna back. I couldn't. She was mine now.

She belonged to me.

Enzo watched me pace the length of the small kitchen. "We may not have any other choice," he told me.

I shook my head. "No."

"Tristan—"

Slashing my hand through the air, I cut him off. "Don't. It's not happening, Enzo. It'll never happen." Before he could argue more, I turned to him. "Would you give Sera back? Wait," I stopped directly beside him, my mouth curving into a sneer as I looked down at him. "You did give her back. You allowed her to be married off to Luigi, an old man with a shriveled dick." I was being a *bastardo*, but he deserved it. He'd given up the woman he loved because he didn't think he was good enough for her. I knew I wasn't a good man. But the difference between us was that I didn't give a fuck if Luna deserved better than me.

"He was the boss. And that was a different situation. Stop trying to change the subject."

"Luca kidnapped Veda and held her hostage in his house to get revenge on his brother. I don't remember him being worried about any strife his actions caused within the family."

Enzo was on his feet. "Stop. None of this has anything to do with what's going on now with you and Luna."

I stepped into him until our faces were only an inch apart. "It has everything to do with it. The only reason you're so freaked out is because this time it's me."

He met my gaze. "I'm not going to deny it," he told me. "If that's what you're waiting for. I love you, T. You know that. But you're one seriously fucked-up bastard. And I just want to make sure I'm not going to come in here one day to find strips of her flesh hanging from the ceiling."

His words made my blood run cold. Not because I wouldn't do something like that. I would. His fear wasn't unreasonable. But I would do it to someone else. Not Luna. I couldn't envision hurting her, no matter what she did or said. "She's safe here. With me. I swear it to you. Now stop being a *stronzo* and get the fuck out of my house."

Enzo searched my face, and I knew he still didn't completely trust me, but he wanted to. Taking a step back, he picked up his sunglasses and put them on. The tension fell from my shoulders once his eyes were hidden. "Okay. I'll go. But I'll be back to check on her."

"That's not necessary. I can take care of Luna."

I expected him to argue with me again, but he surprised me. "Okay," he said after a long pause, and nodded. "Okay. But we'll need to get a game plan together. Gino will be looking for her, and he'll come here. You know he will. We need to have our stories straight."

"I'll come by the house in the morning."

He headed toward the front door. "Thanks for the drink."

"You're welcome. Now go home to your wife."

A hint of a smile softened his hard features. "I'll see you in a few hours."

Locking the door behind him, I pressed my back against it and stared down the hall toward the back room. Was it wrong of me to bring her here? No. I was helping her. Was it wrong of me to lock her in a cage? I rolled the question around in my head, trying to see it from the point of view of someone who'd never had to go to extremes to protect themselves.

Possibly.

But I wasn't wrong about wanting to keep her safe. And right now, that cell was the safest place for her, whether she knew it or not. Gino would never stop looking for her, and he'd tear the city apart to get her back under his control. She wasn't safe out there. Here, I could keep her hidden. Keep her safe.

Pushing away from the door, I removed my jacket and draped it over one of the chairs. Then I set the stove to preheat while I gathered the ingredients to cook for her. When I was finished, I picked up the plate I'd prepared and a glass filled with filtered water, turning off the lights with my elbow on the way to the back room. I had more questions for her, but mostly I just wanted to see her again. It occurred to me that I could do that whenever the hell I wanted to now. I didn't care if she raged or screamed or cried or cursed me.

With her presence calling to me like a moth to a flame, I went to her without pause, reveling in the feeling of the flames licking at my soul.

Perhaps they would burn away this obsession I had with her.

CHAPTER 2

Luna

After Enzo left, closing the bedroom door without a word, I rushed the bars, shaking the fucking things until I nearly pulled my arms from the sockets. I knew it wouldn't do any good, but I couldn't stop myself. When they wouldn't budge, fear rose up inside of me, twisting and turning in my gut until I thought I was going to puke.

Exhausted and still reeling from the effects of whatever the hell kind of drugs he'd given me, I stumbled back a few steps and fell hard on my ass. I looked down at the natural wood pattern of the floor in a sort of stupor, then I shivered as the A/C kicked on, cooling the fine sheen of sweat that covered my face and arms. Why was it so fucking cold in here? Scooting backward, I found the blanket I'd dropped and wrapped it around my shoulders. It wasn't a bed, but at least it was soft and warm.

I don't know how long I sat there, huddled beneath the blanket on the floor, when the bedroom door opened again and Tristan came in carrying a plate and a glass of water. He glanced over at me briefly, then set them on the small table by the lamp before leaving again.

My stomach growled loudly, and I rose to my feet, a little more gracefully this time. Whatever it was, it smelled fucking delicious. Or maybe I was just really hungry.

The door opened again, and this time he had a pair of handcuffs. I watched him approach the cell.

"Put your hands through the bars."

I eyed the cuffs in his hand distrustfully. "Why?" My voice was dry and scratchy from screaming.

"Because I'm going to handcuff you to them so I can bring in your dinner."

"You don't have to do that. I won't try anything. I promise."

"Hands," was all he said.

I was tempted to refuse, but the food smelled so good, and he hadn't done anything to physically harm me. Not yet.

Was that steak?

I blew out a hard breath. Fuck it.

Pulling the blanket up around my shoulders more so it wouldn't fall off, I walked up to the bars and stuck my hands through them.

Tristan closed a cuff around one wrist, and then the other, just tight enough that I couldn't slip out of them, but not so tight that they hurt. But instead of bringing in my breakfast, he gently took my fingers and turned my hand so it was palm up. Then he did the same to the other one. "What did you do to your hands?"

Tearing my eyes away from his face, I glanced down at my hands. My palms and fingers were bright red from gripping the bars so hard. "I tried to break out," I confessed without shame.

I felt, more than saw, the way he stiffened. "Why did you do that?"

"Because I don't want to be in here. I don't want to be your fucking prisoner."

His dark eyes clashed with mine. I tried to read what he was thinking, but of course it was no use.

"You're not a prisoner," he told me. "You're my guest. Don't try that again."

I didn't bother to argue with him, but he was fucking crazy if he thought I was just going to happily live my life in this cage for his amusement. Then I almost laughed, because he *was* fucking crazy. Anyone who locks another person up in a cage has some serious issues. I just hoped he could handle his better than Gino.

My silence seemed to bother him, but eventually, he pulled a key out of his pocket and unlocked the door to the cell. Then he picked up the plate and the glass of water and brought them inside, setting both on the floor just inside the door. My eyes followed that plate of food as far as I could. It *was* steak. And little baby red potatoes.

"Do I have to eat off the floor like an animal?" I asked him, staring straight ahead again. The floor was actually really clean, as was the bathroom. I wondered what the rest of the house looked like. Or was it even a house? I mean, I assumed it was, but for all I knew, I could be in the middle of a warehouse or something, like a fish in a fishbowl.

"For now. I apologize that this room isn't more comfortable."

He sounded distracted, and I noticed he didn't offer to do anything to *make* it more comfortable for me. Against my better judgement, I peered over my shoulder. Tristan was still sitting on his haunches, and he was staring at the floor behind me. I tried to see what he was looking at, but it was impossible with my hands cuffed to the bars. With a sigh of impatience, I faced forward again. "What are you staring at?"

The blanket was yanked from my shoulders, and I jumped. "Hey!" His hands were on my arms, feeling down my back and sides to my ass and legs. I tried to kick him. "Stop it!" I told him. "Get your hands off me!"

My efforts to get him away from me were useless. "Why is there blood on the floor?"

That got my attention. I stopped kicking. "What?"

"Blood," he repeated. "There's blood on the floor. Are you on your period?"

My face burned at his blunt question. "No." I didn't know why I was embarrassed. My menstrual cycle, and every other woman's, was perfectly natural and not something I was usually shy about. Especially not in the industry I worked in.

I stepped to the side, trying to avoid his hands, when he suddenly grabbed my ankle and lifted my right foot off the floor. I heard him curse softly.

"What?"

"You didn't tell me you were hurt."

I thought I caught a hint of anger in his tone. Instinctively, I tried to pull my foot out of his hand when he probed at the cuts with his finger. I'd totally forgotten about my barefoot run through Gino's yard, such as it was, with all the rocks and burs in lieu of grass. But now that he mentioned it, the bottoms of my feet did sting now that I was getting more feeling back into my body.

Gently, he set that foot back on the floor and picked up the other one. After he poked and prodded at that one, he put it down and said, "I'll be right back."

I startled. He'd stood up silently and was now directly behind me, his voice tight. Leaving the cell, he locked me in. "Wait!" I called. "Don't leave me here like this!"

He showed no sign that he'd heard me, walking out of the bedroom without a backward glance and closing the door behind him.

"Dammit." I rattled the cuffs against the bars and looked longingly at my meal growing cold on the floor. "Tristan!"

But then he was back, and in his hands was what looked like a bottle of peroxide and a tube of something, along with some bandages. He let himself back into the cell, locking it behind him. "Give me your foot," he ordered.

"My feet are fine. I'll rinse them off and clean the floor after I eat."

"Luna."

A tingle ran through me at the way he said my name.

I heard him exhale. "Please let me clean those cuts so they don't get infected."

If they did, would he bring a doctor to treat me? That just gave me all the more reason not to comply.

"I know what you're thinking," he told me. "But it wouldn't work. Our doctor is paid well to keep his mouth shut and forget what he sees as soon as he leaves. He wouldn't dare try to help you get out."

Knowing I was pushing my limits, and not wanting to find out what would happen if I pushed him too far, I rolled my eyes and lifted one foot behind me.

He lowered himself to his haunches and set down the supplies he'd brought. Then he gently took my ankle in his hand.

"Thank you," he told me.

I tried to ignore how warm and gentle his fingers were as they held my foot in the air, cleaning out the cuts and applying the salve. Tried not to remember the way those fingers had felt exploring my body. But by the time he wrapped the bandage around my foot and tapped my ankle so I would give him the other one, my chest and face were warm, and my breathing was erratic. I tried to play it off like he was hurting me, but I didn't know if I succeeded.

He didn't say a word as he tended to my sore feet. And when he was done, he went into the bathroom and came out with a wet cloth that he used to clean the floor.

I had the insane urge to apologize to him for making a mess, but caught myself before I could. Why the hell should I? I never asked to be here. Never asked him to save me.

But if he hadn't, you'd probably be right back at Gino's by now. Hell, you might even be dead.

I shut that voice down. It might be true. It might not. It didn't matter. I was a prisoner here. At least with Gino, I had the illusion of still having a choice.

He took the washcloth with him when he left the cell, locking me in before he removed the cuffs. "Eat." He nodded toward the food he'd left on the floor for me.

This time, I didn't even pretend to fight with him about it. Hobbling a bit on my bandaged feet, I sat on the blanket and pulled the plate of food and glass of water toward me.

Outside of the cage, Tristan lowered himself to the floor, crossed his long legs at the ankles, and leaned back against the wall across from me.

I ignored him. If he got off watching me eat, then he could have at it. I was fucking starving. Picking up the fork, I stabbed a bite of the pre-cut steak and brought it to my mouth. It was touching my lips when I paused and pulled it away, eyeing it like the red meat had suddenly turned into a snake.

"Do you not like steak? I don't make it often, but it's good for you to eat after being through a traumatic experience."

"I love steak," I told him as I turned it and looked at all sides. "I'm just wondering if it's drugged or poisoned."

His voice was cold when he said, "I would never contaminate your food, Luna. If I wanted to drug you, I'd stab a needle into your throat again. And if I wanted to kill you, I would pull out my gun and do it. Poison takes too long, and I wouldn't make you suffer like that."

Weirdly enough, I believed him. Shoving the meat into my mouth, I tried to chew it slowly because *good god,* this was the best fucking steak I'd ever had in my life. But it actually took me about three or four bites before my stomach was satisfied enough to allow me to enjoy it.

"Do you like it?"

I glanced up over at him. His expression was inscrutable, and he sat so still he could've been made of stone. But I thought I caught a glimpse of something in his eyes before it was gone, like shutters had been pulled down to hide his thoughts from me. "It's really good. Thank you."

His shoulders relaxed, and he crossed his arms over his chest, seemingly content to sit quietly and watch me eat. When I was finished, I pushed the plate and half empty glass away and leaned back with a sigh, mimicking his pose. I had to admit, having a set of steel bars between us made me much gutsier than I normally felt when he was in the same room with me. "So, now what?"

He tilted his head. "Now I want you to tell me what happened between you and Gino that made you so desperate to get away from him you didn't even stop for shoes."

I frowned. My head had been a little muddled, but I specifically remember telling him that Gino had come in with a gun and that I'd bit him. "I already told you."

"You told me an abbreviated version. I want the entire story."

I lifted my chin. "Let me out of here, and I'll tell you whatever you want to know."

His eyes burned holes in my skull. "I'm not going to do that."

"Then I'm not going to tell you." I held his stare. He could try to intimidate me all he wanted to, but I wasn't going to just sit in here and let him pull all the strings. He narrowed his eyes on me, and I let my gaze wander over the artwork on the walls, changing the subject. "What's with the drawings?"

Apparently, he had no qualms telling me whatever the hell I wanted to know. Without taking his eyes from me, he said, "You're a beautiful subject. I like to draw you."

I pulled my legs in, crossing them in front of me and leaning forward. "You get that it's creepy to have so many drawings of me, right?"

"Why?"

"Why?" I repeated. "Because it is."

He cocked his head. "It took me a few times to get the shape of your face right." Looking around at the artwork on the walls, he narrowed his eyes and shook his head. "I'm still not completely happy with them, but I'll get it."

"Tristan, these drawings are amazing. Creepy, but amazing. They don't even look like drawings. They look like photos." The compliments burst from me before I could stop them. But it was true. He truly had a gift.

"Are you finished eating?"

I looked down at my empty plate and panicked. I didn't want to be left alone again. Trying to keep the desperation out of my voice, I said, "Yes, thank you. But why don't you stay and talk to me for a while?"

"About what?"

"Well, I don't know anything about you."

"You know more than a lot of people."

"What does that mean?"

Instead of answering me, he rose from his position on the floor like a jungle cat, full of strength and grace that I would never possess. I stiffened when he pulled the handcuffs out of his back pocket and approached the door to the cell.

"Hands, please."

"Tristan, seriously. You don't have to do that. I swear I won't try to run off. Or touch you." I scooted back into the corner furthest from the door. "See? I'll stay right here."

He watched me warily, but didn't put the cuffs away.

"Please. I swear." The first step to escaping was to get him to trust me.

I didn't think it was going to work, but then he put the cuffs back in his pocket and unlocked the cell door. Without taking his eyes from me, he came in and removed the empty plate, setting it outside the door and leaving the water. Then he turned and his eyes roamed over my face before dropping down to my body and back, darkening with something I couldn't name. After a moment, he closed and locked the door, closing himself inside with me.

My heart began to pound as he stalked me like the predator he was, waiting for the right moment to pounce. By the time he did, my nerves were stretched so taut I almost screamed when he dropped to his knees in front of me, but I managed to stay where I was. I refused to show him any fear if I could help it.

But what he did next surprised me. "Face that way." He lifted his chin toward the opposite wall of bars. Swallowing hard, I adjusted my position until I was facing away from him. He took my braided hair in his hands. It was a tangled mess, half of my hair not even in the braid anymore, but fixing it hadn't been my first priority.

"What are you doing?" I asked when he removed the tie at the bottom and began to unweave the braid.

"Don't move. Stay exactly as you are." The rumble of his deep voice, so close and intimate, raised gooseflesh on my skin. Loose hair tickled the sides of my neck as he gathered it up in his hands, pulling it away from my back and shoulders. Carefully, he ran his fingers through the strands, gently detangling the knots as best he could. I didn't move. I couldn't. The tension between us was so thick my muscles were frozen in place and I had a hard time breathing. Was I the only one who felt it?

When his fingers were able to move through my hair without getting snagged, he let it fall naturally down my back. The heat of his body warmed my skin as he leaned so close, his chest brushed against my shoulder blades when he inhaled. "I love the way you smell," he said softly. "That was one thing I couldn't capture in my drawings. The way you smell. And the way you feel. So soft." His fingers trembled as they trailed up my arms.

I closed my eyes, fighting the arousal he forced out of me so easily. "Are you going to keep me in here forever?" Was that his plan? To keep me locked up so he could play with me whenever he wanted? Like a doll?

Once again, his answer surprised me. "No. At least, I don't think so." He continued to run the tips of his fingers up and down my arms, raising more gooseflesh.

All my focus was on that soft touch, and I had to give myself an internal shake to remember what we were talking about. "You don't think so?" I repeated. "When will you know?"

"When you're safe. When I have you out of my head." He sounded distracted as he smelled my hair.

"You still haven't told me what you're trying to keep me safe *from*. Maybe I wouldn't fight you so much about being in here if you'd just tell me."

His touch disappeared, as did the warmth of his body close to my back. Slowly, I turned to face him, making sure to keep my hands to myself. He was sitting back on his heels, his entire body tense, watching me warily. We were so close our knees almost touched. I slid my ass back on the floor, putting a little more distance between us.

"Tell me," I demanded.

CHAPTER 3

Tristan

"Gino is your father." I hadn't planned to blurt it out like that, but there really wasn't a way to break the news to her gently. And she was right. She deserved to know why I'd brought her here. I'd never planned to keep it a secret.

Her large blue eyes blinked once. Twice. "What did you just say?"

"After your mother was killed, you were given up for adoption. You and your brother. It was Gino who turned you both over to the state." I searched her face. Her eyes. The way she held her body. Trying to understand what she was thinking. How she was taking all of this. But I couldn't read her.

She sat very still. Too still. "How do you know about my mother?"

Ah, that was a question I wasn't ready to answer. Not yet. "She was the wife of a capo in *La Cosa Nostra*," I told her. "Gino's. Your biological father. They had two children. You and your younger brother, Logan."

She gave her head a little shake, struggling to understand. "I was with my...my *father*?" Looking anywhere but at me, she shook her head again. "No. That's impossible."

From her reaction, I knew what I'd said before to Luca was correct. She didn't remember him. I wanted to hold her hands, to comfort her, but instead I dug my fingers into my thighs. "Luna, your current situation with him wasn't your fault. You didn't know."

"But you did? And you're just telling me this now? After all the times you snuck into my room?" Her voice was calm. Without emotion. But she flung her hand out, gesturing at the drawings on the walls. Proof that I was there, just like she said.

"I didn't know who he was to you right away. And when I found out, I came to get you immediately."

"To save me."

There was no sarcasm, but still, her words didn't sit right with me. I was no hero. But I also couldn't allow her to stay there, knowing what I did. "It wasn't right for you to be there..." *Fucking him.* It was what I wanted to say, but I couldn't bring myself to say the words aloud.

She stared at me for a long, long time. And then she started to laugh.

I drew back, surprised, and unsure how to react. I was prepared for her anger. Her tears. Violence, even. Why was she laughing? "Do you understand what I'm telling you, Luna?"

"Oh, I understand," she burst out when she'd caught her breath. "I understand I just tried to bite...I can't even say it!" With that, she lost it completely, throwing her head back and laughing until tears were rolling down her cheeks.

What the hell was wrong with her? "You did what?"

She waved my question away, gulping at the air like a fish out of water.

"Luna." I watched her closely as I rose to my feet. She was acting unpredictably, and it was making me nervous. I backed toward the door and put my right hand in my pants pocket, wrapping my fingers around the key, ready to escape if I needed to.

"I'm sorry," she gasped, one hand pressed flat to the middle of her chest above her breasts. "I'm sorry. That's just the funniest fucking thing I've ever heard in my life." The smile that lingered on her lips fell as she stared at the floor. "Mostly because it's not funny at all, if you think about it."

"It wasn't a joke."

Her eyes flicked up to meet mine, then she wiped them with the heels of her hands. But I saw the uncertainty reflected there before she looked away again. "It's got to be a joke. Or, or, an excuse to kidnap me and lock me up in here. I was nine when our mom died. Old enough to remember my father."

"Okay. Then tell me, what do you remember about him?"

She sniffed as she dropped her eyes back down to the blanket in front of her, then she pulled it over her lap and rested her elbows on her knees. "Not much," she admitted quietly, still staring at the blanket.

I wished I was able to blank out my past the same way. Unfortunately, I remembered everything.

When she raised her eyes, the mirth was gone, her normally animated face expressionless. "Do you lock up a lot of women in here, Tristan?"

I let her change the subject, knowing she needed time to process what I'd just told her. "No."

"Men?"

"No."

"Then why do you have a cage in your house?" She paused, looking around. "This *is* a house, right?"

"Yes. It's where I live."

"So, why the cell?"

Should I tell her? I hesitated. But then she met my eyes, and there was so much desperation in her gaze I found myself confessing. "It's for me."

She blinked in surprise. "For you?"

"Yes."

"They lock you up in here? Why?"

I shook my head. "No one else is involved."

Her brows furrowed, little lines forming on her forehead. "You lock yourself in here."

I wanted to smooth them away and make her laugh again. "Yes."

The lines grew deeper. "Why?"

My eyes traveled the perimeter of the cell, taking in the iron bars, the hard floor, and the thick blanket. "Because it's safe in here."

"Safe," she repeated. "Who are *you* hiding from?"

I couldn't hold her gaze and looked away. I suddenly didn't want her to know about this part of me and my life. It would make me appear weak to her. And I wasn't fucking weak. Not when it came to Luna. I would protect her against her demons—and mine—if it came down to it.

"It just might help me to understand if you told me." The words were spoken so softly they were nearly a whisper. "So, please, tell me."

My stomach was in my throat. A giant lump I couldn't speak past.

"Tristan...please."

I closed my eyes. I couldn't resist the plea in her voice. But I still couldn't speak. If I showed her what had happened to me, what I was now, would she believe me to be a monster? Or a victim? Somehow, the second one was more abhorrent to me. I shook my head. No. I couldn't show her.

She was quiet there in her spot in the corner. Waiting.

My mind spun. But would she stop fighting me if I showed her? Stop trying to escape? Would showing her my scars help her to trust me? To understand why she needed to stay here? With me?

Taking a deep breath, I calmed my thoughts. Then, with my eyes still closed, I unfastened the buttons of my shirt. I felt the weight of her stare crawling across every inch of skin I exposed. Heard her steady breathing now that her fit of laughter was over. I tried to concentrate on that. On her scent that filled the room. And tried not to think about what would happen when she saw. However, as more and more of my scars were revealed, I listened for her gasp of horror. For the pity that would fill her voice when she told me how sorry she was that this had happened to me.

But neither of those things happened. My shirt was open halfway to my navel when my hands stilled and I opened my eyes to find her staring at my bare chest with wide blue eyes. It was enough. I dropped my hands to my sides, where they tightened into fists.

Carefully, she stood on her bandaged feet and limped her way over to me until she was less than two feet away. Her eyes met mine before they dropped back down to my chest. She reached out her hand and I slammed into the bars behind me. "Don't—"

"I won't touch you."

Drawing in a ragged breath, I held perfectly still as she took the edge of my shirt between her thumb and forefinger and pulled it aside. I knew what she was seeing—burn scars where cigarettes had been extinguished on my skin, ragged pink welts where I was whipped with belts and chains, missing chunks of skin and muscle that had been cut out of me, and the jagged edged lines I'd left there myself with the dull edge of my knife. There was only the slightest catch in her voice when she asked, "What happened to you?"

Although I'd been expecting the question, it was a moment before I could speak. And when I did, my voice was strained. "It was part of my training."

She frowned. "Training for what?"

"To be Luca's personal guard."

Her eyes met mine and my heart stopped, my breath freezing in my lungs. This close, the blue of her eyes, ringed with black, had wisps of cobalt deep within their depths, like threads of a story waiting to be told with every shared glance. And I wanted to know every single detail of that story.

"Do all of you have to go through this?"

Still lost in her eyes, I shook my head. "No. Just me."

She broke eye contact, once again studying my scars, and I blinked hard a few times, sucking in air. "Why just you? Why not everyone?"

"I..." That was a question I used to ask myself often, but not anymore. "I don't know. I was given to Luca's father as a child, and he made me into what I am now."

"A killing machine?"

"Someone who would give his life without thought to protect the boss' son." Her body's proximity to mine was fucking with me. I felt trapped with the bars against my back. She was too close, and she smelled too good. My mouth watered to taste her, and my heart raced. Yet, at the same time, adrenaline flooded my system, urging me to run.

"What about you?" she asked, meeting my eyes again.

"Me?" I asked, confused.

"Yeah. Who protects you?"

I stared into her eyes, drowning in the depths as the horrors of my past fell away. I felt like she could see right through me, and I tore my eyes away before she discovered how truly depraved I was. "I don't need protection. I've survived on my own for a long time."

She tilted her head, her long midnight hair sliding to one side like strands of silk, her expression a mixture of curiosity and concern. "Survived? Or just existed?"

I hesitated, a flicker of vulnerability burning inside of me for just an instant before I extinguished it. "Does it matter?" I shifted against the bars, the cold steel reminding me of the harsh reality I lived in. A reality she didn't belong in.

However, as she stared me down, I sensed a quiet understanding I hadn't expected, a shared acknowledgment of the less than perfect pasts we'd both survived. "Needing someone to lean on doesn't mean you're weak, Tristan. It just means you're human."

A bitter smile teased the corners of my mouth. "In this world, leaning on someone gets you killed. If you want to survive, you can only count on yourself."

Her eyes held mine, unwavering. "Maybe there's more to life than just surviving."

"Do you really believe that?"

She shrugged. "I'd like to. Wouldn't you?"

The question lingered between us, like an unspoken challenge. And in that moment, the weight of my position in this life made my bones feel heavy. But breaking free from the chains that bound me was impossible. Nor would I want to, even if I could. I didn't know anything else.

Yet, as she stared up at me with eyes that were far from innocent and somehow still full of hope, a seed of doubt took root in my mind. In the way she looked at me, I saw a glimpse of something I'd never allowed myself to believe in—a chance for redemption.

No. That was impossible. Not even a blue-eyed temptress who tasted like sin and had a heart large enough for the both of us could save me now.

I stepped to the side, pulling my shirt closed and buttoning it. But my hands were trembling so much I couldn't get the tiny buttons through the holes. Our conversation had me out of sorts. I felt unsteady on my feet. Unsettled. And I didn't fucking like it.

"Here, let me help you." Luna moved in front of me again and reached for my shirt, but I grabbed both of her wrists, stopping her. Her lips parted in surprise and, without thought, I took her mouth with mine, kissing her hard. I knew we needed to talk more about what happened with Gino. I needed to make her understand why I'd brought her here. But right now, all I wanted to do was drown in the taste of her until her moans in my ears overpowered the voices in my head.

Turning us around, I raised her arms above her head and said against her lips, "Hang onto the bars."

She did as I told her without question, reaching behind her and wrapping her fingers around the cold metal, her eyes on mine and her chest rising and falling with fast, shallow breaths.

"Don't let go." Slowly, I released her hands and pulled the handcuffs out of my back pocket. I had to get even closer to cuff her wrists to the bars, and as soon as it was done, I found myself instinctively retreating, my muscles tense, my senses on high alert for any hint of danger. But I quickly calmed down when the handcuffs clanged against the metal bars, reassured that she was under my control.

Jesus fucking Christ, she looked so damn fuckable with her lips swollen from my kiss and her hair falling in messy waves around her shoulders. A red flush crept up her chest as my eyes wandered down to her full breasts. Her pink tank top was so thin I could see the darker color of her areolas and the hardened peaks of her nipples. My groin tightened, and I licked my lips. I wanted to taste them.

Stepping close, I was about to take out my knife like I had last time when I remembered she didn't have any other clothes here. Although I would enjoy having her naked at all times, I knew it would make her feel too vulnerable. So, instead, I lifted her shirt from the bottom, exposing her soft stomach as I raised it up and over her breasts, exposing them completely to my avid gaze. I moaned aloud as they rose and fell with each breath. And in response, she closed her eyes and let her head fall back against the bars, arching her back.

With a shaking hand, I skimmed my palm over one nipple. Luna jerked once before settling back against the bars. With both hands this time, I lifted and kneaded her breasts. I loved the weight of them, soft and firm and giving all at once. Lowering my head, I sucked one nipple into my mouth, rolling it around on my tongue and scraping it with my teeth. Luna whimpered, and I moved to the other side, sucking and tasting before kissing my way to her stomach.

Dropping to my knees, I pulled her shorts down and waited for her to lift one bandaged foot, then the other. I left them on the floor beside us and sat back on my heels. Soft dark curls hid the delicate pink flesh of her sex, and I ran my fingers through them, feeling the texture before I opened her wide with my thumbs, pressing her hips to the bars with my palms. When that wasn't enough, I lifted her right leg and laid it over my shoulder. My skin shifted restlessly where she touched me, but I blocked it from my mind and focused on the sight and scent of her. Again pressing my palms against her hips, I used my thumbs to expose all of her to my hungry eyes.

"Tristan..."

My name was a moan on her lips. She was wet and ready, but I made myself wait, savoring the anticipation until she was squirming against my hold and raising her hips to my mouth. Then, and only then, I lowered my head and lapped up the moisture with my tongue. God, she tasted so fucking sweet. I listened to the sounds she made, focusing my attention on the areas she seemed to enjoy the most, my cock growing uncomfortably hard.

I relished the pain. Craved it. Just like I was beginning to constantly crave the feel of Luna's skin beneath my fingers and the taste of her on my tongue.

Burying my face in her pussy, I shoved two fingers inside of her, groaning when she tightened around them. With my other hand, I unfastened my slacks and pulled out my swollen cock. I pumped my length, fucking her with my fingers and tonguing her clit.

She made the most beautiful sounds as she ground her sex against my face.

Her cries mingled with my moans as my fist tightened around my cock and I pushed my fingers in deep, sucking her clit into my mouth and flicking it with my tongue. She came hard, her weight heavy on my shoulder as her standing leg gave out.

My own orgasm slid down my spine, tightening my balls, slamming through me as I threw my head back with a cry. My cum coated my hand and the bars of the cell, covering the floor outside of it.

When I could breathe again, I gently lifted her leg from my shoulder and lowered my forehead to the juncture between her thighs, my hands gripping her full hips to hold myself steady. The musky sweet scent of her was stronger now, and I forced my tongue between her folds, licking her from back to front as far as I could reach.

I'd never in my life experienced a connection with someone like I just did with Luna. I didn't even know how to describe it. It made me wonder what it would feel like to come inside of her. But as I imagined myself on top of her, her arms and legs wrapped around my naked, scarred body, the heat in my blood suddenly turned to ice. "I'm sorry. I have to go."

I couldn't look at her as I tucked myself back into my pants and stood. Locking her in the cell, I quickly un-cuffed her hands, leaving the metal bracelets hanging from the bars by one cuff. Luna calling my name was the last thing I heard as I rushed from the room in a panic.

Later, much later, I would wish with everything in me that I'd stopped and turned around.

CHAPTER 4

Luna

No! Please! Stay with me!

I'd called after my new jailor like some kind of pathetic about-to-be-ex girlfriend just because he'd gotten me off. What the hell was the matter with me?

My hands shook as I yanked down my tank top and picked up my sleep shorts from the floor, then stalked into the bathroom to wash his scent from my skin, slamming the door behind me.

Wetting my hair, I reached for the shampoo and froze. Everything in there—the shampoo and conditioner, the body wash, the razor, even the loofah—they were all the exact kind I used every day. Same brand. Same scents. Everything.

Holy shit. Bringing me here wasn't some spur-of-the-moment decision like he'd claimed. No. He'd fucking planned this. How long had he been watching me? And at what point did he decide he was going to take me for himself?

And when, exactly, had I stopped thinking of him as my kidnapper and started craving him as my lover?

I groaned aloud, telling myself I'd only called out like that because I didn't want to be locked up in here alone again. But as I scrubbed my skin raw trying to remove the memory of his touch, I knew it wouldn't do any good, because this psychopath had somehow dug his way *beneath* my skin, like a fucking parasite.

I suddenly stilled, bent over with one leg only half washed, the loofa dripping soap onto the shower floor, as I realized that I hadn't even tried to block him out this time. Nope. I'd been extremely aware of every touch of his fingers. Every brush of his lips. Every lick of his tongue. Every sound he made as he explored my body and made me come harder than I ever had in my life.

It didn't make sense. All I knew about him was that he was extremely dangerous, and extremely damaged. I mean, yeah, he was good looking. But a lot of men I knew were. So, what made this one different? Why was he in my head?

As I wrapped a fluffy white towel around myself, I spotted the cell phone he'd given me on the counter.

I could call Logan. He would help me get the hell out of here. I was pretty sure I was on Luca's property, because I remembered seeing a small house through the trees as we'd driven down the drive to the main house the day of the wedding. It would make sense that the mafia boss would keep his most trusted guys close.

Grabbing the phone, I started tapping in my brother's number. But I hung up before it could ring. What the hell was I thinking? My younger brother couldn't just storm the stronghold of a mafia boss armed with a textbook and his righteous indignation and demand they release his sister. He'd be shot before he found the house. If Tristan didn't kill him—and I completely believed he'd carry out his threat—one of Luca's other guards would gun him down the moment he stepped foot on the property. And I seriously doubted they'd take the time to ask questions first.

Tears filled my eyes as I set the phone back on the counter and finished drying off, wishing I had clean clothes to wear. Preferably something that covered me a little more. After combing my hair, I put my shorts and tank top back on and sat down on the closed toilet seat because it was better than sitting on the cold floor. Wiping the tears from my eyes, I hit redial. Logan didn't answer, so I left a message letting him know I'd gotten a new phone and to save this number. I told him I'd talk to him soon, and put the phone back on the counter. Then I forced myself to think about what Tristan had told me before I'd turned the conversation around to him.

My stomach churned, and I stood up.

Standing in front of the mirror above the small sink, I stared at my image, trying to see if I had any features that could've come from Gino. It was hard to tell by the shape of our faces, because he was older and had some extra weight on him. My eyes were large and blue, his were brown and squished between his ample cheeks and his heavy brow. My hair was so dark it was nearly black. His, what was left of it, was salt-and-pepper gray.

My little brother's image came to mind, but Logan looked a lot like me. Same dark hair and blue eyes, only his skin wasn't as pale as mine. It was darker with the olive tones of Italians. Like Gino's.

I huffed out a breath. No. It wasn't possible.

But...what if it was?

I didn't want to believe it. I really fucking didn't. But no matter how hard I tried, I couldn't remember the man who'd been married to my mother. I knew he was Italian. But that was all. He was hardly ever around when Mom was alive. And after she'd died...

Well, the last thing I remembered from that time of my life was running into the living room and seeing my mother's body on the floor, bright red blood staining the white carpet beneath her. Her eyes were filled with horror, and her mouth was open on a silent scream. And she was looking right at me and Logan.

I shoved the memory away. I didn't like to think of my mother like that. I preferred to remember her smiling, her eyes glittering with life as she chased us around the yard or wove bedtime stories about princes and princesses trapped in castles with dragons.

Covering my mouth with one hand, I choked back a sob. I tried to imagine the vivacious woman I knew as a child with a man like Gino, but I couldn't. However, if what Tristan had said was true, that made the events of the last few months make a whole lot more sense in a weird sort of way. The bet he'd made at the poker game. How he'd taken over my finances—and Logan's—without blinking an eye. And the way he'd been acting while I lived in his house. How he'd acted almost guilty when we'd...we'd...

My stomach revolted and I bent over the toilet, flinging the lid open just in time. Oh, my god. Had I been fucked by my own biological father? Sucked his cock? Walked around on his arm like one of his whores in front of his associates?

Much as I tried to deny it, I kept thinking about how he'd acted around me. How he only came to me after he'd been drinking. How he seemed confused sometimes when we talked, like he thought I was someone else. Someone from his past.

Logan's been telling me my entire life how much I look like our mother. He still tells me that sometimes, and he still gets sad because I remind him so much of her.

Those times when Gino talked to me like I was someone else, did he think I was...

Her? My mother?

"Oh, my god." Propping my elbows on the toilet seat, I held my head in my hands.

It couldn't be true. It couldn't be. I had copies of the paperwork from when Logan and I had been put into the foster system. If we were Gino's, wouldn't we have his last name? Gone to live with a family member if he didn't want us? Something?

I'd always assumed my mother didn't have any family that would be able to take us in. But I did wonder about our father often, especially the first few years after she'd died. I'd never heard anything about what had happened to him, and kind of always assumed he'd died that day, too. It was better to think that than to know he just hadn't wanted us anymore.

"Luna?"

I lifted my head and a thrill of excitement shot through me before I realized that wasn't Tristan's voice. I frowned at my reaction.

"Luna? Are you okay?"

He sounded genuinely concerned, so I got up off the floor and rinsed my mouth with water and mouthwash before coming out of the bathroom. My eyes immediately went to the floor outside of the cell, but the evidence of

Tristan's last visit had been cleaned up while I was in the shower. My face burned when I saw Enzo standing just outside the cell, looking both formidable and inscrutable in his expensive suit and dark sunglasses.

Oh, god. Had he cleaned up the mess Tristan left? I didn't really want to know. "What do you want?" I asked him sullenly.

"Tristan asked me to let you know that he had to go do something and he'd be back in a few hours."

Picking up the blanket, I wrapped it around my shoulders. "Why the hell would I care if he's here or not?" It's not like I wanted him around, unless it was to release me from this godforsaken prison.

Enzo stared at me a moment, then reached up and removed his sunglasses.

I'd never seen him without them, not even at his wedding, and the effect was startling. His deep brown eyes were so expressive, I could read every emotion. Every thought. And right now, he was worried.

"Has he been treating you well?"

I laughed out loud. "In case you haven't noticed, I'm locked in a cell."

He exhaled impatiently through his nose. "He has his reasons, Luna."

I approached the bars. "Oh, yeah? And what reasons are those, Enzo? Because he's a psycho who's been stalking me?" I flung my hand out, encompassing all the drawings covering the walls. "Did you know that? Did you know he's been stalking me? And now he's locked me up in a cage so he can do God knows what to me?"

"He won't hurt you." I knew he was trying to be reassuring, but he didn't sound completely convinced.

"How do you know?"

"Honestly, I don't," he admitted after a pause. "But he's never acted this way before, so I have to believe that he won't."

"Acted what way?"

"He's never"—he looked away for a moment before his eyes came back to me—"...cared before. About anyone except Luca and me."

"If he *cared* about me," I mocked, "he wouldn't have me locked up in here. That doesn't make sense."

"It makes perfect sense in Tristan's mind. He's trying to keep *you* safe in the only place that's ever kept *him* safe."

"That's what he keeps telling me," I admitted. "But, personally, I think he's full of shit."

He studied me for a moment. "He's fed you, correct?"

Reluctantly, I nodded.

"And you have everything you need?" He gestured toward the bathroom.

"I don't have any clothes."

"I'm sure he'll rectify that as soon as he can."

I didn't respond.

"So, he *has* taken care of you."

My face flamed again at the double entendre, and I ducked my chin, not answering.

"Look..." He took a step toward me. "I know this is asking a lot of you, Luna, but just...try to be patient. Tristan will let you out when he knows it's safe. I mean, you should really be a little more grateful."

My head shot up, and I was surprised balls of fire didn't shoot from my eyes. "*Grateful?*"

The corners of Enzo's lips turned up and his expressive eyes twinkled. The fucker was baiting me.

"Either let me the hell out of this cell, or go away," I spit out between clenched teeth. My patience was at an end. I was cold. I was bored. And I was getting hungry again.

"I can't let you out. I don't have the key."

"There has to be a spare somewhere."

But he shook his head. "I'm afraid not."

Defeated, I backed away until I felt the wall against my back and slid down to the floor, pulling up my knees and wrapping the blanket around my legs and bare feet. I was so tired of being cold.

Enzo was still watching me.

"So, what is it with him?" I asked in a dull voice. "I mean, I know he's fucked up in the head, obviously. But why does he lock himself in here?"

Enzo was quiet for so long, I didn't think he was going to answer. And when he did, his voice was carefully controlled, but there was a flare of raw pain in his eyes for his friend. "Tristan was abused by Gino when he was a child."

Gino was one of the men who did those things to him? An acidic taste filled my mouth.

"I'm sure you've seen his scars by now?"

I nodded. "Some of them."

"Well, there're more on the inside—a *lot* more—that he keeps hidden. He doesn't even know that I'm aware of what happened to him. Luca, too. But we let T keep his secrets. We don't want him to feel ashamed for things that happened when he was too young to stop it."

"What *did* happen to him, exactly?"

He dropped his eyes to the floor, dark lashes shielding them from my view. "Gino raped him when he was a child," he finally said. "More than once." He met my horrified stare. "Many times, actually."

Holy shit.

Enzo pulled his sunglasses out of his inside coat pocket and put them on, hiding himself from me again. "It was the only thing that got any kind of real reaction out of him. The physical torture was something he quickly learned how to block out. But not that." Restless now, he approached the cell and wound his hands around the bars in front of him until his knuckles went white. "When he was a child, he was kept in a cell much like this one. Iron bars. Hard floor. Cold. One blanket, not as nice as that one." He paused, and though I couldn't see what was going on behind the dark glasses he wore, I could hear the compassion he felt for his friend in his voice. "Gino didn't have a key to the cell. Only Luigi, Luca's father, had that key."

I was beginning to understand. "So he was...safe when he was in his cell."

"Yes. Luigi only pulled him out during specific hours of the day to go through his *training*." I could hear the disgust in his voice now. However, it quickly changed to pride when he spoke again. "But Tristan was strong. Stronger than any of them knew. And he would fight them. He'd fight them so hard that Gino, who was in charge of all of that shit, would feel like Tristan needed to be reminded that he was nothing to them. That his life, his feelings, meant nothing. He 'put him in his place,' I heard him say once." His upper lip lifted in a sneer, and his voice was thick with disgust. "And his place, according to Gino, was underneath him."

Bile rose in my throat. "That's why he doesn't like to be touched."

Enzo nodded. "We're not sure what exactly triggered that repulsion—the physical abuse, the sexual abuse, or both—but it's the way he's been since he got out of there and came to work for Luca."

"How old was he when this was happening? And where the hell were his parents?"

"He was six or seven when he first went to live at Luigi's. T was given to him by his father, who was one of the capos. I'm not sure of the details of that transaction. The physical portion of his training lasted until he was a teenager. The abuse from Gino stopped as soon as Tristan was big enough to fight him off. And by that time, Tristan had gone from being a shy, skinny kid to a killing machine that couldn't be stopped by threats or even bullets. Nothing scared him anymore. I've seen him step right in front of a gun to protect Luca without a second's hesitation. I've seen him chase someone down with multiple bullet wounds. He doesn't think about what he's doing. He doesn't get scared. He doesn't feel anything. He just does what he was created to do. What he's told." He cocked his head, and I could feel his eyes studying me behind the dark glasses. "Until you."

"I'm not sure how I should feel about that," I said, my throat thick with tears for the little boy Tristan had once been. I understood what it was like to have your body used by men. How it made you disassociate, because you couldn't stand the feel of your own skin.

"I didn't tell you all this so you could feel sorry for him," he told me. "I'm telling you this to help you understand, because I don't think Tristan would ever try to explain, or if he'd even be able to. And to ask you to have a little patience with him."

I wasn't a completely cold-hearted bitch. I had plenty of empathy for the man, knowing what I did now. But I couldn't promise anything else, so I didn't respond.

Enzo cleared his throat and took a few steps back from the cell, pulling his composure around him like a shield. "Do you need anything? Other than clothes? I'll talk to Tristan when he gets back, or see if Sera has something you could borrow."

"I would appreciate that." I tried, and failed, to keep the sarcasm from my voice. I knew I'd gotten myself into this by not screaming the first time he'd shown up in my room. By making that bet against Gino to begin with and living up to my word. Not that I would've had a choice. Knowing what I know now, I'm sure if I'd tried to back out, Gino would've just taken me and locked me away, too. I'd be in the same situation I'm in now.

And just like Tristan, no one would've tried to stop him.

CHAPTER 5

Tristan

Luna was curled up in the corner of the cell when I returned. She had her knees pulled up to her chest, and the blanket wrapped tightly around her. Her long, dark hair was confined in a thick braid that fell over her shoulder, but the ends were unravelling without a tie. Her head rested against the wall, her eyes closed. But I could tell she wasn't sleeping. Her face was too tense.

I was glad she wasn't waiting for me with her questions. It gave me a few seconds to take her in and enjoy her, the way I did when I snuck into her room and watched her sleep. "I brought you a few things."

She gave no indication at all that she'd heard me.

Taking the keys from my pocket, I kept my eyes on her while I opened the door and slid the duffle bag I'd brought her into the cell before closing and locking it again. I wasn't ready for any more contact. Not yet. "I couldn't bring everything, so I only took what I thought you'd be most comfortable in."

Nothing.

"Are you upset with me because of the way I left earlier?" I tried to think of a way I could explain to her. "I'm sorry…"

"No," she interrupted. "You're not." With a heavy sigh, she opened her eyes. "Don't say it if you don't mean it."

I'd been hearing that a lot lately.

"And no. I'm not upset about the way you left. I'm upset because I'm still in this fucking cell. And I'm bored. And I'm hungry. And I'm cold. And I have nothing warmer to wear."

"You do now." I nodded toward the bag. "And I'll make you something to eat."

"That still won't fix my biggest problem."

"No," I agreed. "It won't. But it's all I'm going to offer right now."

Moving stiffly, she got to her feet and walked over to the bag on her bandaged feet. She opened it, then reached inside and started pulling out clothes. Leggings, T-shirts, a sweater, socks. And her cotton underwear and bras. "You got my clothes."

"Yes."

"You broke into my room at Gino's?"

 I wasn't sure why she sounded so surprised. "You needed your things. I can go back for the rest tomorrow if you'd like."

"But..." She straightened, a pair of leggings in one hand and underwear in the other. "Why would you do that?"

I frowned, trying to figure out where she was going with this line of questioning. "You needed clothes, Luna."

"Yes, but why not just get me new clothes? Instead of risking going back to Gino's?"

Oh. "I thought you'd be more comfortable if you had your own things. Would you prefer new? Do you need something else?"

She glanced down into the bag and then back up at me, an inscrutable expression on her perfect face. "No. No. This is great. It's exactly what I would've packed had you given me the chance."

For once, there was no anger in her tone. Not even a bite of sarcasm.

"What is it?"

"Nothing." She pulled a few more things out of the bag. Something was wrong. There was something I'd missed.

"You're lying to me, and I'd like to know why. Was there something else? I can go back."

She shook her head. "There's just a picture." She glanced up at me, trying to act nonchalant, but I could see in her eyes that she was upset. "It's me and my brother when we were kids. The only one I have of us. Our foster father destroyed the rest when I left."

I wracked my brain, but I didn't remember seeing a picture. It was obviously important to her, though, so when I could, I'd go back and get it for her.

Dropping the clothes back into the bag, she approached the bars until she stood directly in front of me. "Tristan, please. You don't have to keep me in here."

I stared down at her, and it was on the tip of my tongue to apologize again, but I caught myself. Because she was right. It wouldn't be sincere. I said the words because I knew people liked to hear them. It made them feel heard. "Yes, I do," I said simply. She still didn't understand. This was the *only* safe place for her right now. The cell kept her safe.

And it kept her contained and under control. No surprises.

She opened her mouth to say something else, but I held up my hand, turning my head slightly toward the open bedroom door. Vehicles were coming up the drive. "I'll be right back."

"Tristan, wait!" She grabbed for me through the bars, and I quickly stepped back out of her reach. Her fingers curled into a fist. "What is it? Where are you going?"

"Luca has visitors. I need to go see who it is."

"Is it Gino?"

Her tone was difficult for me to discern. I stepped as close as I dared. "He can't get you in here, Luna. Even if he finds you, he can't hurt you."

For one second, there was something in her eyes. Sympathy? That didn't make sense, but it was there and gone before I had the chance to know. Perhaps I was only imagining things.

"He could shoot me. He doesn't have to be in here to do that."

"He'd have to get through me first." And it was at that very moment that I knew I would step in front of a bullet for her. That somehow, she'd joined the very short list of people I would protect with my life.

Wrapping her arms around her middle, she retreated from me until she was out of arm's reach. She didn't seem reassured. Instead, she appeared shaken.

"I'm going to lock you in. If anyone besides me or Enzo comes in here, hide in the bathroom until I get back."

After a brief pause, she nodded. "Okay."

I met her eyes briefly as I closed and locked the bedroom door behind me. I didn't think Gino would harm her if he somehow managed to get into this house without my knowing about it, but I wasn't about to take any chances. Then I took both keys and locked them in the safe in my room. In the kitchen, I moved the blinds aside and looked out the window, catching the taillights of a black sedan going around the curve to Luca's. Gino's car. I'd beaten him here by only a few minutes. Was he here for Luna? Or for me? For breaking into his house?

Only one way to find out.

Grabbing my jacket from the back of the chair where I'd left it, I put it on and locked Luna inside the house.

By the time I arrived at Luca's, everyone was gathered in the great room, just inside the door. I quietly closed the front door behind me and stood in front of it, blocking the exit. Luca was directly across from me, Enzo to his right and a step behind him.

Gino and three of his men stood with their backs to me. I had no reaction to being so close to one of my childhood abusers. I'd learned to shut off anything I felt toward him or the others years ago.

Luca was speaking. "—why you think she would come here."

Gino put his hands in the air, palms up. "I don't know where else she would go. She's not with her brother. I've had my men following him for the last twenty-four hours.

She's not there. And your boy is the only other person she's spoken with since she's come here." It wasn't an accusation. Not quite. But the implication was there.

"Perhaps she's hiding in his—" Luca glanced around, searching for an answer on the walls. "—apartment? House?"

"Dorm," Gino answered. "He's in college."

"Dorm, then," Luca said.

"She's not there. We searched the building."

Luca lifted his eyebrows. "The entire building?"

"I'm very thorough."

Crossing his arms over his chest, Luca studied him. "Maybe you should just let her go."

I couldn't see Gino's expression, but I saw the way his shoulders drew back. "That's not an option. She owes me a debt, and she hasn't paid it off yet."

Luca looked around him to me, standing silently in front of the door. "Tristan, have you seen Luna? She appears to be missing."

"No," I answered immediately.

"There." Luca shrugged one shoulder. "We haven't seen her."

"I'd like your permission to search your house. And his." He glanced over his shoulder at me.

Luca's expression hardened, but he didn't move a muscle or raise his voice. "That's not going to happen. She is not here."

Enzo's hand went to his gun as Gino's men did the same.

Gino laughed a little, looking around at the circle of men. "Please, please. No need for dramatics. But I think a search is necessary, Luca. You have a big place. She could be hiding somewhere, and you wouldn't even know it."

"As I said, that's not happening."

"How will I know for sure she's not here if I'm not allowed to have my men take a look around?"

Luca didn't budge. "You're going to have to take my word for it." It was a simple request, but everyone heard the underlying threat. Luca was the boss. Doubting his word was a very serious offense. He'd been extremely patient with Gino up until now, but his patience was at an end.

Gino returned Luca's stare, and then he gave him a nod. "If you see her, or hear anything, I'd appreciate it if you'd let me know."

"Of course."

Moving carefully, Gino turned to take his leave. When he saw me standing in front of the door, he smirked. "Get out of the way, boy."

I glanced at Luca, waiting for his nod before I moved to the side and allowed them to leave. Opening the door for

Gino and his men, I watched him walk out to his car. Something was definitely going on. He walked as though someone had cut off his balls.

Narrowing my eyes, I remembered the blood on Luna's chest and the stained neckline of her tank top when I'd grabbed her mid-escape from Gino's yard. She'd told me he had a gun, and she'd bitten him, but she hadn't told me where.

The world around me turned red as I imagined what he was doing to have her mouth that close to his cock. His own fucking daughter.

My hand went to my gun as the car drove off, the tires kicking up a few rocks that were on the pavement.

"Tristan. Come in here, and close the door, please."

Luca's order sifted through my murderous thoughts, but it took me a few seconds to obey. Closing the door, I walked over to him and Enzo. The buzzing in my head was loud, and my teeth were clenched so hard they hurt, but I did as I was told.

"Where is Luna?" Luca's bright blue eyes burned through the lies on my tongue.

I didn't answer him.

"Tristan. Tell me where Luna is."

"What makes you think I know?" I finally said. Not a lie, exactly. But not the truth.

I expected him to ask me more questions the way he always did, but apparently his patience was up with me, too.

Walking around me, he ripped open the front door.

"STOP." My gun was in my hand, and it was pointed at Luca's head.

"T. What the fuck are you doing? Put the gun down!" Enzo was in my ear, but I couldn't hear him past the hoard of red-eyed demons screaming in my head. I needed to protect Luna. And nothing and no one was going to stop me.

Luca stopped short in the doorway and slowly turned. When he saw the gun pointed at him, he stepped back inside and shut the door. "You have her."

I didn't respond. It was none of his fucking business.

"Where is she?" he asked. "Tied up somewhere? Or locked in your cell?"

"Luca?"

I glanced toward the stairs. Veda stood frozen halfway down the stairs, one hand on the rail. Her eyes were wide, and her voice shook with fear.

Never taking his eyes from me, Luca tried to reassure her. "Everything is fine, *amore*. Go back upstairs. I'll come up when Tristan and I are done talking."

She didn't move, and I cocked my head at Luca.

"Enzo, please get Veda back upstairs so T and I can talk."

From the corner of my eye, I saw Enzo take a step closer to me. "Do not pull that fucking trigger," he ordered.

"It's fine, Enz. Go with Veda."

I didn't lower the gun as we waited for Enzo to get her out of the way. From the commotion I heard on the stairs, she didn't go easily, and he ended up practically carrying her back up the stairs and into Luca's room.

When we heard the slam of the bedroom door, Luca inhaled and exhaled through his nose as he studied me. Throughout everything happening with Veda, he'd never taken his eyes off me. "Are you going to shoot me, T?" he asked softly.

"Honestly? I'm not sure." It was true. Luca was probably the closest thing I'd ever had to a brother, but right now, there were no feelings of family loyalty keeping me from taking him out if he decided to come between me and Luna.

He nodded slightly. "Fair enough. Can you tell me *why* you're on the verge of shooting me, then?"

That was a very good question, and I wasn't quite sure of the answer. I'd acted on impulse when I'd pointed the gun at his head, and it didn't sit well with me. But I also didn't put it away. "You're not going to my house."

"Because Luna is there."

There was no point in lying now. "Yes."

"Did she come to you and ask you to help her?"

"No. I took her from Gino's."

Unperturbed by the gun pointed at him, he rubbed his forehead with the fingertips of one hand, the other went to his hip. I wondered if he really trusted me not to shoot him or if he was just going by the rule to show no fear. "Jesus Christ, Tristan."

"I had to get her away from him. I have to keep her safe."

Both hands on his hips now, he studied me. "Other than the fact that you went against a direct order, which we'll deal with later, this..." He trailed off and shook his head, sighing heavily. "Tristan, this is going to cause us a lot of problems I'm not ready to handle yet."

I lifted the gun another inch, so it was pointed directly at the center of his forehead. "You're not taking her back to Gino. She's not going back there."

His eyes were hard. "You can put the gun down, T. I'm not going to take her anywhere."

"I want your word."

"You have it," he said without hesitation. "I won't do anything we haven't agreed upon together." Then he laughed, but it was an ugly sound, and his eyes went to the ceiling where Veda was currently being contained in their room. "Besides, who am I to talk?"

He was right. He'd had us kidnap Veda right out of her sister's apartment. The sister he was *supposed* to take. And even when he found out he had the wrong woman, he refused to give her up. She'd fought him at first, just like Luna was doing with me, but eventually, she'd fallen in love with him.

Was that what I wanted? For Luna to love me?

I wasn't sure I even knew what that meant. Love. The concept was completely alien to me. Until I came to Luca, the only kind of human interaction I'd ever known from another person had left bruises and scars on my body. And on my soul. I tugged on the knot of my tie with my free hand, trying to loosen it and get some air. Sweat dripped down my spine and my heart was racing out of my chest.

"T."

Luca drew my attention back to him.

"Put the gun away, my friend. Or just go on and shoot me, if you must. But make a choice. You're beginning to make me nervous." He smiled, but it didn't quite reach his eyes.

I lowered the gun and returned it to its holster. "I'm sorry."

His smile grew. "No. You're not."

"You're right. I'm not."

He huffed out a laugh. "Alright. Let's talk about Luna."

"There's nothing to talk about."

"I'd like to see her."

My entire body tensed. "You don't think I can take care of her?

He shook his head. "No. That's not it at all. I just thought it would be helpful if I reassured her that we don't mean any harm."

"She knows. She's not happy about being here," I admitted. "But she knows I'm not going to hurt her."

I thought he would press the subject, but he didn't. "Then let's talk about Gino. Eventually, he'll be back."

I narrowed my eyes. "That's it?"

"The damage is done, T. Nothing I say or do will change that. I'm not happy with you, but we have bigger things to worry about right now."

And that's what made Luca a good boss, and a good friend. He was direct, and he almost always kept a level head. "He has no proof that we have her. Even if he went to the rest of the capos or one of the other families, no one would help him without proof. Especially not against you."

"I think it would be wise to be prepared. Just in case."

I nodded. "Luca."

His eyes met mine.

"You know you can trust me. Despite what happened here today, I would never put you or your family in danger."

"I know. But sometimes a woman makes a man act in ways that aren't his nature. So next time, before you pull a gun on me, take a moment to step back and think about what you're doing."

"Does that help?"

He gave a derisive laugh. "Hell, no. Women make us fucking *impazzito*." Crazy. "Speaking of which, let me go reassure Veda I'm still alive. Why don't you go into my office? Enzo and I will be there in a moment so we can discuss how to handle Gino with this."

I watched him jog up the stairs before I turned and headed down the hallway to his office. I already knew how I was going to handle Gino, the first chance I got.

He would never hurt Luna, or me, again.

CHAPTER 6

Luna

Tristan didn't come back for two days. He had Enzo bring my meals, all homemade and delicious. I was going to get fat eating all this food without getting any exercise, but I didn't even care. Maybe if I made myself unattractive enough to him, he'd let me go.

Even the girl in the drawings seemed to smirk at me at that one.

At lunch on the second day, I asked Enzo offhandedly where the food was coming from.

"Tristan makes everything for you. He doesn't trust anyone else."

I was surprised. "Tristan? Really?" That meant he was here. He was just ignoring me. Maybe the novelty of having a real-life doll in a cage was already wearing off.

"He's a very good cook," Enzo told me as he collected my tray. He never cuffed me to the bars. And he always left the cell door open when he came in. But trying to escape never even crossed my mind, because I knew I'd never make it out of the room.

"I noticed," I said distractedly. My mind wandered back to the meals that had appeared as if by magic in my room in Gino's, and a warm feeling spread through my chest. It was Tristan who'd left them there for me. It had to be.

I wasn't sure how to feel about that.

"Why is he making you bring my meals to me?"

Tray in one hand, he locked the cell door and paused. "He's working through some stuff. It's best to just let him do it."

"Well, thanks for not letting me starve."

"You're welcome, Luna." Then he left, shutting the bedroom door.

Getting up off the floor, I started doing my twice daily walks around the cell, trailing my fingers along the bars as I went. One thing I did appreciate about these guys, they were always straightforward with me. At least, as much as they could be. There was no sneakiness or beating around the bush. Unlike Gino, who always seemed to be hiding something from me.

Because apparently, he *was*.

As I'd been doing ever since Tristan dropped the news on me of who Gino really was, I pushed the thought out of my head. I wasn't ready to dive too deep into the reason he felt he needed to bring me here. Because when I did, I was so filled with disgust I wanted to sanitize myself with bleach, inside and out. It wasn't a good head space to be in, so I stayed out of it. For now.

When I got tired of walking, I texted my brother on the cell phone Tristan had given me. I could call him, but I wasn't sure that I'd be able to fool him into thinking I was happy, and I didn't feel like fending off his questions. Luckily, we chatted like this a lot, so he didn't think anything of it. He texted back right away. He was on a date.

My eyebrows rose, my own situation temporarily forgotten.

A date with who???

LOL No one you know, sis. Just a girl I met in class.

What's her name?

Cadence.

That's a pretty name.

A pretty name for a pretty girl.

> !!! Come on, little brother. You've got to give me more than that.

> No. I don't. Night, Luni. I'll tty tomorrow.

I FROWNED DOWN at the screen. Fine.

The bedroom door opened, and I looked up to find Tristan in the doorway. For a moment, my heart forgot to beat, and I went hot and cold a few times before I stuck to hot.

He was wearing a white button-down shirt with the top two buttons undone, black slacks, and dress shoes. No jacket. As always, his appearance was impeccable. The scent of a waterfall in a dark forest drifted to my nose, and my lower stomach tightened in response.

His eyes immediately went to the phone in my hand, and I answered the unspoken question I saw there. "I was just texting my brother. Checking in."

"And how is he?"

"He's on a date," I told him in disbelief.

"Is that so hard to imagine?"

I sighed and glanced down at the phone again before setting it in on the bathroom sink. "I guess not," I admitted as I came back out into the cell. He was still standing in the doorway. "Where've you been?"

He didn't answer right away. "I had some things to deal with."

"That's what Enzo said. What kind of things?"

Sliding his hands into the front pockets of his black slacks, he studied me in that intensive way he had. His eyes didn't seem quite as lifeless as they had when I'd first met him, or maybe it was just wishful thinking on my part. "It's hard to explain."

"Can you try?" I told myself I was only asking because I was so damn bored, but in some small, hidden part of me, I knew that wasn't true. He seemed upset, and it bothered me. Not that he gave any physical indication. It was more of a feeling I had.

He looked away for a moment before bringing his eyes back to me. "You told me the night I brought you here that you bit Gino to get away from him."

The terror of that night slammed into me out of nowhere, and my eyes filled with tears as I wrapped my arms around myself, suddenly cold despite the leggings and long-sleeved shirt I was wearing. I blinked them away. A reaction that wasn't missed by Tristan. "Yeah."

"Where did you bite him?"

I frowned. "Where? We were in my room."

"No. On his body. Where did you bite him?"

Gino's roar of pain filled my ears, and I could suddenly taste the salty copper of his blood on my tongue. "I'd rather not talk about it."

He took another step toward me. "What was he doing, Luna, when you bit him?"

I shook my head. *Nothing I want to talk about.* "I told you, he had a gun."

"Did he have his cock in your mouth?"

Pushing stray hairs off my face nervously, I didn't answer him. Was this why he'd been ignoring me? Did he feel some strange sense of betrayal because he'd snacked on my pussy a few times?

"Luna."

There was an unspoken command in his tone, but I just shook my head again.

"When Gino came here looking for you the other day, he walked in a way that led me to believe he had an injury in an...inconvenient place. And I want to know if it was you who gave him that injury."

I didn't know how to answer that question. I couldn't read him, and I sure as hell had no clue how he would react if I told him the truth.

"I need to know, Luna."

I met his stare with a mutinous one of my own. "Why? What does it matter?"

It was his turn to get caught off guard, and it took him a minute to respond. "I don't know. But it does." He paused. "Please. Tell me."

Though his expression remained unreadable, there was something in his tone. Vulnerability, maybe? And before I knew what was happening, my mouth opened and the words poured out of me before I could stop them. "He came into my room, and he was drunk, and he had a gun in his hand. I thought he was going to shoot me. Or himself. Or maybe both of us. So I distracted him the best way I knew how. I gave him a blow job to buy myself some time."

If my admission bothered him at all, he didn't show it. "And why did you bite him?"

"Because...because he put the gun to my temple, and I didn't know what else to do. So I bit him hard enough to draw blood, and then I climbed out the window and I ran."

The muscles of his jaw moved, like he was clenching his teeth.

Shoving the horror of that night deep down into my nightmares where it belonged, I dropped my arms and walked up to the bars, wrapping my hands around them and pushing out my breasts. "Would you like me to do that to you? Would you like to feel my mouth around your cock, Tristan?"

A spark of hunger flickered in his eyes, but it was quickly followed by a flash of anger. "Don't do that."

"I'm just asking." I ran my tongue along my lower lip, wetting it.

His eyes flicked down to my mouth and then came back to mine. "Don't," he repeated. "You don't have to play the whore for me."

"Isn't that why I'm here? So you can handcuff me to the bars and molest me whenever you feel like it?"

"No."

"No?"

"No. That's not why you're here. You're here so I can keep you—"

"Safe," I finished for him. "Except there's only one problem with that answer."

"What problem is that?"

"I'm not yours to protect."

He drew back at that. Not physically. Physically, he didn't move a muscle. Didn't even blink an eye. But I felt it, the way he pulled away as he took in my response and rolled it around, trying to decide how it made him feel, and deciding he didn't like it.

We stared at each other for a long time.

It was me who broke the silence. "Look, I understand why you did what you did. And it's not that I don't appreciate the gesture, even if I don't agree with the way it was carried out. But you can just let me go now, Tristan. I can go to my brother's. Or I can get him and the two of us can go somewhere else. Start a new life."

"Gino won't let you go that easily. He would hunt you down and he would find you."

"I know how to make myself disappear. He wouldn't find us." I leaned into the bars and used his own word against him. "Please. You can just let me go."

His voice was strained, pain and confusion thickening his tongue and darkening his eyes when he said, "No. I *can't.*"

What little hope I had drained out of me, and I was suddenly exhausted. Because, at that moment, I knew I wasn't leaving this place. I was stuck here in this damn cell, and who knew if I'd ever see the sun again. Or my brother's handsome face.

And that last thought was what broke me. Hot tears filled my eyes and spilled onto my cheeks, and I turned away. I couldn't look at him anymore. I couldn't stop the wrenching sobs that burned my throat and made my chest ache. My life may not have been the greatest life, but it was better than being locked away when I hadn't done anything wrong.

I didn't hear the turn of the lock or the opening of the cell door, but suddenly Tristan was in front of me. His hands cupped my face, forcing me to look up at him. His dark eyes burrowed into mine, seeing right through to the pain deep inside, and for a moment, I thought he was angry with me.

"What the fuck are you doing to me?" he whispered. Then his mouth crashed onto mine.

I tasted the saltiness of my tears and the sweetness of iced tea as he kissed me hard. Kissed me violently. His short mustache and beard rough against my tender skin.

As the heaviness of my emotions spiraled into desire so fierce that it threw me off balance, I grabbed onto his arms to steady myself, digging my fingers into the muscles of his forearms through his crisp, white shirt.

Tristan stiffened, groaning like an injured animal. Breaking off the kiss, he pressed his forehead to mine, his ragged breaths warm on my face as the tips of his fingers dug into my skull. But he didn't push me away.

It took a second for my lust-filled mind to realize what I'd done. I immediately released his arms, my hands floundering in the air for a minute, not knowing what to do or where to go, until I finally tucked them under the hem of my shirt. "I'm sorry," I breathed. "Shit. I'm so sorry. You surprised me and I just..." The horrific, nearly inhuman sound he'd made echoed in my ears, and I knew it would haunt me for the rest of my life. I'd never heard anything so filled with pain and fear and helplessness.

I held perfectly still, his uneven breaths hitting my face. I didn't know what else to do or say, so I just waited, my heart breaking for this man who was once a little boy who'd been so horribly abused that years later something as simple as the touch of another person would send him spiraling back to that place. I didn't want to be here, but I didn't want to hurt him either.

"I want you to touch me," he confessed. "So fucking bad." The words were said so quietly I wasn't sure I'd heard him correctly. "Fucking hell, Luna." He lifted his head slightly, but he wouldn't look at me. "Jesus fucking Christ."

"I'm sorry," I said again.

"It isn't your fault."

The pressure from his fingers lessoned and he released me, taking a step back.

Even though he was still within touching distance, I felt his withdrawal all the way to my bones, and it made me want to cry all over again.

His eyes traveled over my face. "I don't like to see you like this."

I wiped the tears from my cheeks, new ones mixing in with the old. "I just hate it in here so much," I told him softly. "I can't sleep. And my entire body hurts from sitting on the floor. But the toilet isn't much more comfortable. Can I at least have a chair? A mattress? A pillow? Something?"

A haunted expression crossed his features. He shook his head. "No."

"Why not?"

"Because I can't change it."

My mind spun, trying to understand. "The cell? You can't change the cell?"

A muscle jumped in his jaw as he gave a quick shake of his head.

So he wasn't trying to punish me by making me live like this. That was something, at least. "Can I come out of the cell?"

"No."

Struggling to keep my cool, I asked, "Why not?"

"Because when you're in here, I know that you're safe."

"But you keep Luca safe, right?"

He narrowed his eyes. After a long pause, he nodded once.

"And he's not in this cell. So, couldn't you keep me safe, too?" I couldn't tell if he was listening to me or not. "You can keep me safe," I repeated. "Even if I'm not in here."

His dark eyes bore into mine. "You'll run."

"What if I swear to you that I won't?" I was surprised to discover that I meant it. I wasn't sure why, but I couldn't seem to stomach the thought of deceiving him. Maybe because so many other people in his life had. And I knew what it felt like to be exploited by the people who were responsible for raising you.

"Why should I believe you?" he asked. "I know you don't understand why I did this. Why I have you in here. I know you don't want to be with me, despite the way your body reacts." His eyes dropped to my puckered nipples, my hips, and back to my face. "No. You'd run again the first chance you got."

"I'm also a woman who keeps her promises," I insisted. "I ended up with Gino because I made a bet and I lost, so I lived up to my promise. I didn't run until my life was in danger, which I think is understandable. I wouldn't break a promise I made to you, either, Tristan. And I swear to you I won't run. I won't go anywhere until you tell me it's safe for me to leave."

"What if I never tell you that?"

"It would still be better than being locked in this cell without anything to do and nothing but a hard floor and a blanket for a bed."

He studied me for a long time. I knew what he was doing. He was looking for tells that I was lying, just like I did when I played poker.

"What do you say? I promise I won't leave this house unless you tell me I can. I'll even come back in here if anyone comes around. And I can help you cook and clean or whatever you want me to do."

His eyes dropped to my lips before coming back up to mine, and I suddenly felt too hot in my long-sleeved shirt and long pants. "I need to go do something for Luca." He walked around me and left the cell, locking me in.

My heart dropped to my stomach, and I had to hold back a sob.

In the bedroom doorway, he stopped. "I'll think about it."

Although my body already ached at the thought of another night on the floor, I guess that was all I could ask. It was progress, at least.

That night I took a tiny flicker of hope to bed with me.

CHAPTER 7

Tristan

My skin tingled and burned where Luna had gripped my arms, and I cursed under my breath as I tried to lock the front door for the third time, but my hand shook so damn much the fucking key kept slipping out of the lock. Jamming it into the keyhole for the fourth time, I finally got it.

What would've happened if I hadn't reacted the way I had? Where else would she have touched me?

I stopped walking and looked over my shoulder, toward the house. Thoughts of Luna consumed me, just like they had every second since I'd brought her here. I gritted my teeth, the tight control I'd always kept over my emotions caging me in as effectively as the bars that held her inside that cell. And just like her, I longed to burst free from the prison of horrors that kept me from what I wanted.

And I *wanted* Luna.

I listened for the soothing tones of her voice everywhere I went, even when I knew she couldn't possibly be there. Looked for the startling cobalt blue of her eyes in the gray winter sky. My mouth watered for the taste of her slick pussy. And after years and years without human contact, I *hungered* to feel her hands on my body, soothing the nightmares that marred my skin.

Would they scare her, I wondered? If I let her see the breadth of the raised scars that covered me? Would she find me disgusting? *Un mostro?* A monster? And if I told her exactly how I'd gotten those scars? Would she run from me?

I narrowed my eyes, a rush of adrenaline making the blood surge to my muscles in preparation for the hunt.

She could fucking try.

Shutting down those disturbing thoughts, I continued walking to the black SUV parked in front of my house. I needed to get my mind off her perfect breasts and sad blue eyes and back into the game. Once I was inside the vehicle, I pulled out my cell phone and texted Luca to let him know I was leaving for a while. Then I asked Enzo if he'd check in on Luna while I was gone. There was something I needed to do tonight, and I wasn't sure how long I'd be.

In the end, my assignment took me longer than I'd planned, and by the time I got home the next day, the sun was setting. As I let myself in, I found Enzo in the kitchen, cooking something on the stove.

Surprised to find him there, I hesitated a moment before I pulled the door closed and unzipped my black jacket and shrugged it off my shoulders. "What are you doing?"

Sunglasses firmly in place, he continued stirring. "I'm making dinner for Luna. I wasn't sure how much longer you'd be." He glanced at me briefly over his shoulder, watching as I laid my jacket over the back of a chair. I felt his eyes roaming over me, looking for injuries, before he said, "How'd everything go?"

"Uneventful. I don't think I'll run into any problems. How is Luna?"

"She's bored, but otherwise okay. When do you plan to go back to take care of things?"

"I'll go tomorrow night."

Enzo nodded.

I eyed him as I made my way to the fridge to get a drink. Something wasn't right. "What?"

"I just have a bad feeling."

I paused with my hand on the refrigerator door. I've known Enzo a long time. He had good instincts, and I trusted them. If he had a feeling about something, one way or the other, I listened. "What do you mean?"

He didn't answer right away, so I got the tea from the fridge and poured myself a glass while he gathered his thoughts. "I don't know. I just have a feeling. The Russians...they're not going to let this go."

"They won't know it was me."

"Are you sure about that?"

I stared him down. No one saw me unless I wanted them to.

He changed the subject. "I'm not sure this is the right action to take."

I didn't answer. "It's what Luca ordered."

"Luca's had a grudge against this particular family since his father had to pull him out of New York because he killed that young Bratok."

"He was causing problems in our territory. It was the expected result. Even the Russians knew that. They didn't retaliate then, and they won't now."

"I never said he didn't deserve it. And they didn't retaliate because Luigi cut a deal, which included sending Luca here." He paused and stirred. "I don't know why Luca is still hanging onto this feud after all these years. He's well established here in Austin. He has Veda. Why's he worried about a few Russians coming to town?"

I shrugged one shoulder. I didn't pretend to understand how Luca's mind worked. And honestly, I didn't care if he wanted to hold a grudge against the Russians. I took an impatient breath, eager to see Luna, and a foul odor filled my nose. I approached the stove warily. "What the hell are you making?"

"No idea. I just threw some stuff together I found in your fridge."

"Is that hamburger?"

"No. It's ground sausage."

"I didn't have any ground sausage in my fridge."

Enzo glanced over at me, one eyebrow lifting above the rim of his glasses. "Huh."

"Why don't you go home to Sera. I can take over here."

Handing me the spatula, he gave me a cocky grin. It was unnerving to see him so quick to smile these days. "I'll see you tomorrow."

Once he was gone, I threw whatever the hell was in the pan into the trash and pulled out what I needed to make a quick quiche. I had dough for the crust already prepared, so I baked that while I prepped everything else.

Once the vegetables were chopped, seasoned, and pre-cooked, I added the eggs, cheese, and cream and let it bake while I grabbed a fast shower. But first, I checked in with Luca, letting him know I was back and would give him a full report tomorrow before asking him if he needed me for anything else tonight. He assured me he didn't, so once I was clean, I took the luxury of donning a pair of black lounge pants and a forest-green, long-sleeved thermal shirt. I needed to work out, but I was tired and hungry so I decided to put it off until the next day. Slipping my feet into a pair of house shoes, I went to check on our dinner.

Luna's scent hit me full force as I entered the bedroom with her dinner in my hand. Blood rushed to my cock as an entirely different kind of hunger set in, and I set her plate down on the table by the lamp. I was going to need both hands.

However, the way she winced as she slowly got up and hobbled over to the far side of the cell, away from the door, gave me pause. She threw a look my way that I couldn't decipher, and her eyes widened as they traveled over me.

I glanced down at myself. "What?"

She gestured weakly at my clothes. "I've just never seen you dressed like that."

"I'm off duty for the night," I said by way of explanation. "Hands on the bars, please."

She blinked at me a few times, then limped up to the bars and stuck her hands through without argument.

"Why are you limping?"

"Because my leg is asleep and my ass is sore from this floor," she said impassively.

"That's the only reason? Your feet are healing?"

"Yes."

I was surprised she didn't start in on me to let her out again. I searched her face, and that's when I noticed the dark circles under her eyes. Her lips were pressed together and there were lines of tension around her mouth. Something flickered in my chest, and the thought crossed my mind that I should bring her something—a mattress or a cot, perhaps—so she would be more comfortable.

But the thought of changing anything in the cell made my stomach twist into knots. I couldn't change anything. It had to stay the way it was. The way it always was. Seeing the way she suffered, however, made me feel...odd.

My heart beating in my throat, I stuck the cuffs back into my pocket and grabbed the key, ignoring the voice that whispered in my ear that maybe she was only fucking with me. That I was a fool to trust her woe-is-me act. But another part of me couldn't stand the thought that she was actually in pain and I did nothing to help her when it was completely within my power to do so.

"What are you doing?" she asked. "Aren't you going to cuff me?"

I swung open the door. "Would you like to come eat at the table with me?"

She stared at me like she couldn't believe what she was hearing. "The table?"

"Yes. In the kitchen."

She blinked at me twice. Then, without another word, she rushed to the door. Still limping, but not as badly as before.

When she reached me, I blocked her exit, tensing as she got close, but effectively halting her. "Luna, look at me."

Her blue eyes flew to mine.

"I need you to swear on your brother's life that you won't try anything. You won't try to leave this house. It's late. And I'm fucking exhausted. And I don't feel like chasing you across the grounds just to throw you back in this cell. So swear it, on Logan's life."

Tendrils of fear darkened her eyes. "I swear."

"You swear what?" I needed to hear the words.

"I swear I won't try to leave."

A heartbeat passed, then another, as I stared into her blue eyes, wishing I could see all the way into her soul. "*Va bene.*" Okay. Stepping out of the way, I allowed her to pass.

She stood frozen in place for a fraction of a second, and then she rushed from the cell, not stopping until she made it to the doorway.

"Straight down the hall, past the living room," I answered her unspoken question.

Hands fisted at her sides, she walked stiffly down the hall, looking into every room she passed. There weren't many. Unlike Luca's monstrous home, this house was small, and I preferred it that way. Two bedrooms, an office, two bathrooms, a living room and the kitchen. My room was down another short hallway. I saw her peer in that direction, and I watched, wondering if her curiosity would take her that way.

I wondered what it would be like to have her in my room. In my bed.

Her steps slowed, but then picked up again as she continued to the kitchen.

Retrieving her plate, I followed, my full attention on the site of her walking away in tight black leggings, even though the hoodie she wore over her gray T-shirt obstructed my view of her ass. Luna had the best legs I'd ever seen on a woman. Actually, she had the best everything.

A vision of her plumped out with age and good food, with gray in her hair and lines around her eyes and mouth when she smiled, came to me out of nowhere. And I suddenly wished I had my drawing tablet so I could capture that image on paper.

I very much wanted to see this future version of Luna. I wanted to see her smile at me like that, the skin around her eyes crinkling and her full lips parting to reveal straight, white teeth. Wanted to see the wrinkles in her face deepen and her hair lighten. She would be so beautiful as she aged.

This longing stirred something deep within me that I didn't recognize, some primal need I'd never experienced before. It disturbed me to my core, because I was unable to comprehend these new desires she'd awoken inside me the first day I saw her. I'd always prided myself on being in control, both mentally and physically. But now this petite woman with her gorgeous legs and long, dark hair had turned my world upside down without even trying.

And now that the dam had broken, I was completely captivated by her. Obsessed. Also, I had no idea what to do about these overwhelming emotions flooding my system. All I knew for certain was I couldn't stand not to be near her, and the thought of anything happening to her was enough to send me into a murderous rage.

Somehow, someway, Luna had unlocked something dark and dangerous within me, something I both feared and craved to unleash.

When we got to the kitchen, I set her plate down at the place to my right. Then I got myself some quiche, poured two glasses of tea, and joined her at the table.

"Thank you," she said when I set her glass near her plate. Scooping up a small bite on her fork, Luna looked at the mixture of eggs and vegetables but didn't taste it.

"It's quiche," I supplied. "It's very good. Try it."

After one more skeptical look, she did, cautiously taking a bite and chewing it slowly. Something warm unfolded within me as her eyes closed in pleasure and she moaned deep in her throat.

I wondered if she'd moan that way with my cock stuffed in her mouth.

"Wow. This is really good," she finally said, taking another bite. Strangely pleased that she enjoyed my cooking, I could only stare at her.

"Aren't you going to eat?"

"Hmm?"

One eyebrow lifted as she looked at me. "Your dinner? Are you going to eat it?"

Picking up my fork, I joined her. We ate in silence for a few minutes, the only sounds the scrape of forks on plates and Luna's little sounds of pleasure, but I wasn't oblivious to her presence. Quite the opposite. The woman beside me demanded all my attention to the point where if someone had walked in and put a gun to my head, I didn't know that I'd notice.

"Can I ask you something?" Luna said after taking a sip of tea.

I tensed, the forced casualness of her tone immediately making me wary, but nodded for her to continue.

"Why did you bring me here? I mean, I get that you want to keep me safe from Gino. But, why me? You don't even know me. Why go through all this trouble for someone you barely know?"

Her eyes were searching as she looked at me, genuinely confused. It was a good question. And one I still didn't have an answer for.

Taking her had been an impulsive decision, to hide her here, where her sick father would never be able to touch her again. I'd acted on pure instinct, without reason or logic.

"I don't know."

"That's not much of an explanation," she pressed.

I put my fork down, leveling her with a look. "Would you rather be back at Gino's? Being raped by your own father?"

She shrank back at my harsh tone, dropping her gaze to her plate. The pale skin above the neckline of her shirt flushed red, and I watched as it crept up her throat and jaw to color her pale cheeks. I instantly regretted snapping at her.

I tried again in a softer tone. "There are things you don't understand. Things I never want you to experience. I couldn't leave you there, Luna." I waited for her to look up. To stop hiding from me. When she didn't, I continued. "I know my methods may not be what you consider normal. But I'm not trying to punish you. I'm just trying—"

"To keep me safe."

"Yes."

She didn't respond, merely nodding as she pushed the last few bites of food around her plate. The silence stretched between us again as the comfortable companionship of a few moments ago disappeared. I searched for something to say to break the tension.

"How's your leg?" I asked.

"Awake now that I've been able to move around some and sit in an actual chair," she answered without looking up, but there was no heat in her tone.

We lapsed into silence again. I noticed she was still playing with the food on her plate, but none of it was making it to her mouth.

"You should eat more, Luna," I admonished gently.

"I'm not very hungry."

I studied her down-turned face, noting again the dark circles under her eyes. She looked exhausted, the toll of captivity showing in her slumped shoulders and lackluster mood. A heavy weight settled over my chest as something akin to guilt gnawed at me, but I shoved it down. I was doing this for her own good, even if she couldn't see it.

I finished eating, and then I gathered up the dishes and quickly washed them, hyper aware of Luna's presence behind me. I heard her chair scrape against the floor, and when I turned back around, she was hovering uncertainly by the table, twisting her hands in front of her.

"What?" I asked her.

She let her arms fall to her sides and lifted her chin. "I don't want to go back in there. Please, Tristan. Don't make me go back tonight."

I stared at her, unsurprised by her response but unsure of what to do. Every instinct I had screamed at me to put her back in the cell, where I knew she'd be secure and I'd be able to get some sleep. But the desperate look in her eyes tore at me.

"Please, Tristan," she said again, her voice soft and desperate. "I swear I won't try to run. But I can't take another night on that damn hard floor. And the boredom is killing me, with nothing to do but stare at those weird drawings of me on the walls all day."

I hesitated, warring with myself. She seemed sincere, but how could I trust her when I knew she didn't truly understand why I'd brought her here? Why I had to keep her safe? Hell, I didn't even understand. I'd never shown this much interest in another person before. Not even Luca and Enzo, the two people closest to me. Of course, I didn't want to fuck either of them.

And tying her to a bed again was much more appealing than handcuffing her to the bars of the cell.

When I didn't respond, she tried again. "You'll be here all night, right? That's why you're dressed like that? So, you'll be able to protect me if anything happens." She took a few steps closer, until she was so close, I could've reached out and touched her. "Please, Tristan."

Against my better judgement, I gave in. "Alright. Just for tonight," I finally conceded. "But if you try to run, Luna, I *will* find you."

Luna's face flooded with relief, and she threw her hands up, gesturing for me to stop talking. "I won't! I swear. I won't cause any trouble, I promise."

I nodded, hoping I wouldn't regret this moment of weakness. "You'll sleep in my room with me. In my bed." The mattress was large. I could tie her to one side so there'd be no chance of her accidentally touching me during the night. It was for her own safety more than my peace of mind.

Something flared in her eyes, but it was gone again before I could decipher what it was. Desire? Fear?

"I thought I could just crash on the couch or something."

"No."

"But that's...I didn't mean I wanted to..."

"Didn't want to what?"

She wouldn't meet my eyes. "Nothing."

"I need to do some work in my office first. You can come sit in there with me until I'm finished. It won't take long." I wasn't about to let her out of my sight.

"Okay."

After a stop back at the cell so she could use the bathroom and get her phone to text her brother, Luna followed me silently back down the hall to the small home office. I sat down at my desk and woke up my laptop while she curled up in the armchair in the corner with her phone and typed out a text.

I tried to focus on what I was doing, but my gaze kept drifting to the woman across the room. Entranced, I watched her read her brother's response, emotions easily flitting across her face, the corners of her sweet lips lifting in a small smile as she answered him.

"How is your brother?" I asked.

Startled, her eyes flew to mine. "Um. He's fine."

I didn't really give a shit about Logan. But I found it interesting to watch the way her face became animated when she talked to him. Almost like a little girl.

Something dark and twisted wormed its way through my gut as she went back to staring at her phone, and I nearly took the damn thing away from her and smashed it into the wall. I wanted her attention on *me*. All of it. But that wasn't acceptable behavior. Of course, neither was locking her into a cell.

Once I made sure the discreet cameras I'd planted while I was gone were up and running, I closed my laptop and stood. "Are you ready?"

Luna, I assumed, said goodnight to her little brother and stood, waiting for me to lead the way. It made me suspicious, this unusual compliance of hers, and I searched her face carefully for any signs of deception, but she was good at putting on a mask when needed. I hated that she felt she needed to do it with me, but I didn't force her to expose herself. Not just yet.

My pulse kicked up as we left the office and walked down the hall to my bedroom. Having her in my private space felt dangerously intimate. Even more so than having my face between her legs. The cuffs that were still in my pocket bounced against my thigh, and I imagined her spread eagle on my bed, completely naked, her wrists and ankles secured to the posts. A buffet of soft skin and wet warmth laid out just for me.

Blood rushed to my cock as anticipation quickened my breath. No matter how tired I was, I couldn't seem to get enough of this woman.

Luna stopped again near the door to her room. "I just want to grab something to sleep in."

"You won't need it."

Her eyes flew to mine. "I think I've changed my mind. I'm just going to stay in here tonight."

"You can sleep wherever you'd like, Luna. But know that the cell won't save you from *me*."

CHAPTER 8

Luna

"But..."

"What did you think was going to happen here tonight? Especially when you ask to sleep in my bed?"

"I asked to sleep on the couch. Not your bed."

Cocking his head to the side, he gave me a look that told me exactly how foolish I sounded right now.

He had a point. It's not like I didn't know he'd take what he wanted from me if I came in here with him.

Isn't it what you want, too?

No. Yes. Fuck, I didn't know.

His dark eyes burned into mine. "Come on." With a lift of his chin, he gestured for me to go to his room.

My feet moved, my body obeying him even as my mind stuttered in confusion. I didn't want this, did I? But some part of me must, because I found myself preceding Tristan down the dark hallway to his bedroom, my heart pounding so hard I thought it was going to break my rib cage. He opened the door and gestured for me to go inside. I hesitated only a moment before stepping over the threshold.

The first thing that hit me was his scent. The room smelled like him—dark and clean and spicy, a hint of his cologne mingling with the masculine, earthy scent that was intrinsically his. Shadows danced across the dark furnishings in the dim light from the hallway. The space was neat and orderly, reflecting his meticulous nature. My eyes were immediately drawn to the imposing bed in the center of the room. Large and masculine, it had a black headboard with cutouts and black posts at the foot. The bedding was simple, done in blacks and grays. He'd be able to tie me in place easily.

My face heated at the thought, even as tension coiled low in my belly.

Tristan's presence was a physical force at my back as he entered behind me. The click of the latch rang loud in my ears as he shut us in together.

Anticipation heated my blood as I eyed the outline of the bed in the darkness, only to be replaced with shards of ice the longer I stared at it. "How many women have you tied to that bed, Tristan?" I don't know why I asked. It was none of my business, and I didn't really want to know. But something inside of me *needed* to know.

"None. I've never been with a woman."

As always, his direct honesty threw me for a second. I blinked in surprise as I continued to stare at the bed, momentarily taken aback by his blunt words. I heard the clink of metal hitting wood and then soft light filled the room. I turned to find the handcuffs on the black dresser behind me where he'd left them. A small lamp illuminated the room. He never seemed to turn on bright overhead lights. Was that a preference or another thing that he carried over from his traumatic childhood?

I put the question aside for now and met his gaze. "What do you mean?" Surely, he was lying. Or maybe he was bi? Had he only dated men until me? Was that why he seemed so fascinated with my body?

There was no shame in his voice when he answered, "I've never been intimate with anyone before you."

I couldn't quite keep the disbelief from my voice. "You're a virgin?" How could that be possible when the man made me come so hard I thought my bones would shatter from the force of it.

He stuck his hands in his pants pockets, glancing down as he said in a rough voice, "I don't know that I would call it that."

Tristan was abused by Gino when he was a child.

Enzo's words came back to me.

Oh, my god.

My eyes went to the handcuffs, and I changed the subject. "You're not going to cuff me?"

His eyes traveled down my body and back again. "We'll see. Take off your clothes, Luna."

"No." My answer was immediate and automatic. I could make excuses for my reaction to him when he had me handcuffed or tied to my bed. I could tell myself that even though my body craved his mouth on me, it was still a form of rape because I was unable to run away. He forced those reactions out of me. But I couldn't just give in to him like this. Like I had a choice.

"I want to taste you again."

I swallowed the whimper that tried to escape the back of my throat.

"Please, take off your clothes. I want to see you."

I was about to refuse again, but then I thought about it. I wasn't bound. If I made him happy, maybe he'd just go to sleep, and I'd be able to get the hell out of here. Fuck my promise to him. I wasn't going to live like this if I had a chance to get away. He looked like he hadn't slept in days. And I'd fucked way worse than a hot Italian guy with death in his eyes who had issues with touching.

Decision made, I took off my hoodie and laid it on top of the dresser.

He backed up a step as I reached around him, his eyes heating every piece of skin I revealed as he watched me.

I reached for the hem of my top, pulling it up and over my head. The cool air hit my skin, making my nipples pucker beneath my bra. Tristan's eyes darkened as they dropped to my breasts, and the tip of his tongue wet his bottom lip. Holding my top in one hand, I reached behind me to unclasp my bra, letting the straps fall down my arms before tossing them both onto a pile beside my hoodie.

His throat bobbed as he swallowed, his chest rising and falling with quick breaths as those dark eyes roved over my bare breasts. I shimmied out of my leggings next, peeling them down my legs along with my panties and socks. Straightening, I added them to the pile of clothes and stood before him, completely naked.

Tristan licked his lips as his gaze traveled down my body, taking in every inch of my bare skin all the way to my toes. "You're fucking beautiful," he rasped. "So perfect."

God, he looked at me like he'd never even *seen* a woman before. Like I was a work of art to be cherished and admired, but not touched. He took his time, memorizing my body, making me feel both extremely vulnerable and wanted as I waited, that now familiar ache blossoming between my legs.

My blood raced and the muscles low in my belly clenched. My eyes locked on his. It took all I had not to look away from his possessive gaze.

"Turn around."

I did as he said, feeling more exposed than I ever had before, and that was saying a lot when I stripped in front of men for a living. But this...this was different. This time, I wasn't in control.

His knuckle slid down my spine and I shivered, but didn't pull away. He moved lower, tracing the curve of my ass. My long hair slid across my back as he gathered the mass of it and let it fall over one shoulder, the ends brushing my over-sensitive nipples. His lips touched my chilled skin, placing hot, open-mouthed kisses along the back of my shoulder.

"Keep your hands where they are."

I tightened them into fists and pressed them against the outside of my thighs.

Soft cotton brushed my naked back as he stepped into me. His arms came around mine and his hands cupped my breasts, thumbs brushing over my nipples. I bit my lip to hold in a moan as pleasure shot straight between my legs.

"I want to fuck you so bad," he growled in my ear. His erection pressed into the small of my back, emphasizing his words. My head fell back against his shoulder as one hand slipped lower, fingertips grazing through my damp curls. He stiffened behind me, but when I did nothing else, he relaxed again.

"Tell me you want me, too," he demanded, his voice a deep rasp in my ear. I whimpered when his fingers found my clit, rubbing it with slow, tight circles. I was already so wet for him.

His nose was in my hair, his breath tickling the back of my neck. "Tell me, Luna."

The combination of his demanding words and his hands on my body had me ready to burst into flames.

"I want you," I gasped. There was no use denying it. My body was already betraying me anyway. If I tried, he'd know I was lying.

He pulled me tighter against him, his body hard and insistent against mine as he pinched my nipple then squeezed my breast.

My fingernails dug into my palms as waves of pleasure shot through me, gradually building until I couldn't stop the pleading sounds coming from my throat. Inching my feet apart, I spread my legs wider, arching my back and pressing my breast into his hand and trying to increase the pressure of his fingers on my clit.

And then, suddenly, he was gone. The warmth of his body replaced by cool air.

"Lie down." His voice was low and urgent. "On your back."

I did as I was told, crawling onto the cold comforter, and then lying down on my back.

"Stay there. Don't move."

I watched him walk over to the dresser. He opened the top drawer and pulled something out.

Ties.

Then he turned off the lamp.

"Leave that on," I told him. I wanted to see him. All of him.

"No." That was it. I knew by his tone there'd be no point in arguing with him.

Coming back to the bed, he positioned me in the center and tied my wrists to the posts above my head. I let him do it, my body on fire for him to finish what he'd started. Then he restrained my ankles until I was spread out before him. When he was done, he straightened and studied his work. "Does that hurt?"

"No," I managed to reply. There wasn't much light, but it was enough for me to see his eyes drop to my breasts, and I couldn't help the way my nipples hardened, aching for his touch. His tongue. His teeth. "You'd be able to see me better with the light on."

He ignored me. Lifting one knee onto the bed, he trailed his fingertips down the underside of my arm. "So soft." His voice was so low I could barely hear him. "I want to touch you everywhere. Taste all of you."

His eyes locked on mine as he reached out to touch my face, his fingers gentle as they traced the line of my jaw, sending shivers down my spine. "Stay here with me, Luna," he ordered. "Don't shut me out."

I wanted to. God, how I wanted to. Because I was afraid. Not that I thought he would hurt me physically, but because I could feel myself being dragged into his darkness.

And I was beginning to like it there.

He continued his touch along the side of my throat, down the center of my breastbone and around the outside of my breast before he released me from his gaze.

His fingers brushed against my nipples, teasing them until they hardened and ached for more, then trailed down my stomach, tracing the curve between my hip bones before diving into the curls between my legs, sliding one finger into the damp heat before he moved on to learn the shape of my leg.

I shifted restlessly on the bed as he continued to explore my calves, my feet, the sensitive spot behind my knee, his hands gliding along my skin with purpose and precision. But he wasn't unaffected. His breathing was loud and fast now, and he moaned every time he found a place he particularly liked.

He explored my body with reckless abandon, his touch both gentle and rough as he learned every curve and texture. My blood rose to the surface in anticipation, sensitizing my skin until even the slightest brush of his fingers sent pulses of pleasure through my body. I let my head fall back against the pillow as he consumed me with the fire of his touch.

"Tristan..." I started to protest when it got to be too much, but he silenced me with a look. Stepping back, his eyes traveled over me one more time before he reached out to stroke the inside of my thigh.

My breath caught in my throat as he straightened and pulled off his shirt.

Good god.

He was a large shadow hovering over me, but I could make out the outline of broad shoulders, lean muscles, and a near-perfect male form. Not too thin. Not too bulky. Just strong, like someone who'd earned that strength, not something created from steroids.

"Please," I begged. "I want to see you."

"No."

"Why not?" I demanded. "You've got me spread out on this bed...tied to this bed...to do—"

"Because I don't want you to see me."

My words stuttered to a stop. "Tristan."

"I'm not turning on the light, Luna."

Unbidden tears suddenly filled my eyes. I just wanted to see him. Why was that so much to ask?

"Don't ask me to stop." His voice was low. Desperate. "It's way too late for that."

I blinked away the tears. "Take off your pants," I told him.

At first, I thought he would balk at taking orders from me, but then he dropped his chin to his chest and undid the tie holding up his lounge pants. With long, deft fingers, he pulled the strings loose as he kicked off his shoes.

I held my breath as he shoved his pants down over his hips and let them drop to the floor, then stepped out of them.

CHAPTER 9

Tristan

I stared down at her, a vision pulled directly from one of my fantasies now lying on my bed.

MY bed.

I thought her presence here would feel wrong. No one had ever slept in that bed besides me, and it had taken me years to get used to not being on the floor. I'd never invited anyone to share it with me. I hadn't wanted to.

Yet, seeing her there, her dark hair splayed across my pillowcases, her full lips slightly parted and her eyes shining with tears and hot with desire, stirred something within me. A possessive, dangerous need I'd never experienced for anyone or anything. She belonged here, belonged to me. I was starting to understand that now.

But this wasn't right. I was a killer. A monster. She didn't deserve to have her brightness tainted with my darkness. I'd tried to purge her from my mind. I'd drawn her, over and over. Drawn every memory I had of her in the short time I'd known her.

If I couldn't have her, I'd surround myself with my memories of her, and hope it would be enough.

But now she was here. So near. So vulnerable. And the monster in me thrilled at the power he had over her. I wanted to join her on the bed, feel her soft skin pressed against the ragged edges of mine, make her come alive with my mouth and hands until she came with my name on her lips. What would it be like, I wondered, to feel her skin to skin?

"Do I scare you, Luna?"

"No."

A lie. I did scare her. But she also wanted me. She hadn't been lying about that.

I skimmed my hand up her side and over her breast to her collarbone, then higher, tracing the delicate veins in her throat. I'd waited for this moment for so long. Imagined it so many times. Being inside of her. Feeling her wet heat squeeze my cock. I was almost...

Afraid.

I knew what the act of sex was about between a man and a woman. Luna's window wasn't the first one I'd watched through. But I'd never understood the force that drew two people together until they were humping like animals. Before now, I'd only experienced sex as a punishment, not this uncontrollable pull, this...*wanting*. This compulsive need to touch her and taste her that consumed my every thought until I couldn't stand the feel of my own skin. Leaning over her, I breathe in her scent, unbidden desire mixed with fear.

"Tristan," she whispered. A shiver ghosted along her skin, and I tightened my grip around her throat, relishing the moment. Not to hurt her, but to feel the connection. To feel her pulse pounding underneath my fingers, fighting to be free. But she'd never be free of me. "Do I scare you now?"

Unable to speak or move, she didn't answer. But that was okay, because I was finished talking.

I kissed her, my mouth hard and rough against hers, enjoying the way she struggled as she fought for breath until she had no choice but to open her mouth and let me in. Only then did I relax my grip on her throat and crawl over her on the bed, but I didn't touch her. Not yet. No matter how much I craved the silken slide of her skin on mine. The warmth of her body.

No, not yet.

With my lips and tongue, I ravaged her mouth until she moaned and began to kiss me back. God, she was sweet. So fucking sweet. I explored every inch, nipping her lips to make them swell and soften, until I knew her mouth as well as I knew my own.

I needed to taste more of her.

Taking my time, I made my way down her body, exploring every curve and hollow. I remembered every sensitive spot. Every place that made her moan and tug against her bondages. I learned where she liked me to be gentle, and where she liked me to be rough. The ticklish spot that made her pull away and just the way to touch her to make her catch her breath and arch into me, her body begging for more, even if she couldn't form the words.

She jerked when I skimmed her clit with the tip of my tongue, hips lifting off the bed to try to get closer to my mouth. Fucking hell, I loved the way she tasted. Loved the smell of her desire. She was so fucking wet already, and I growled deep in my throat, amazed at the way she responded to me. Was she like this with every man she fucked? Or just for me?

Imagining her with someone else, a surge of violence filled me, and I slid my hands under her ass and lifted her to my mouth, determined to replace every other *stronzo's* touch with my own. I'd tied the bonds loose enough to give her enough slack to bend her knees, and she did so now, dropping her knees out to the sides to give me more room between her soft thighs. As I tasted her wet heat and listened to her sounds of pleasure and uneven breaths, I wondered if I'd ever get enough of her sweet pussy.

I slid two fingers inside of her, curling them until I hit the spot that made her fuck them herself. When I felt her muscles tense and my name was on her lips, I kissed her one last time before I rose over her. In the darkness, her eyes were dazed with pleasure and disbelief as she stared up at me.

"Tristan, please," she begged.

"Shhhh." I kissed her, forcing my tongue into her mouth so she could taste herself. "I want to feel you come on my cock," I whispered against her lips.

She whimpered softly and lifted her hips until the tip of my cock brushed against her soft thigh.

I moaned, my breathing ragged, as my forehead dropped to her shoulder.

"Untie me," she demanded breathlessly.

"I can't," I groaned. I wanted to. Fucking hell, I wanted to. At least a part of me did. But the other part was terrified of what would happen if I did. And I wouldn't chance it. Not now. Not when I was about to have everything.

"Tristan, please."

Luna was restless beneath me, her back arching as she tried to get closer to me. Slowly, savoring every inch of skin on skin, I lowered my weight onto her until every part of her touched every part of me. The feeling was more than strange. It was overpowering, and my entire body shuddered. I closed my eyes, overwhelmed by the sensation, and wondering if she could feel my scars. "Spread your legs," I ordered huskily.

She did as I told her, sliding her feet apart as far as they would go with her ankles tied and bending her knees slightly.

I positioned myself until the head of my cock slid down through her slick folds and found the warmest part of her. With a feeling of disbelief, I rolled my hips, pushing against her entrance, but I couldn't get in.

Luna tilted her hips beneath me, and suddenly I was inside of her. I froze, my breath catching and my heart in my throat. But it was just the head. Not far enough.

Pulling back, I tried again, using my shaking hand to guide myself this time. My head swam as I pushed inside her, feeling first the resistance and then the give as she opened up for me, her body adjusting to the invasion of my cock.

I cursed softly. Holy Christ. My mind went blank, and I couldn't move as my cock was tightly surrounded by her wet heat, the feel of her so much more than I ever could've imagined. I didn't know it would be like this. So intimate.

So fucking terrifying.

Instinctively, I started to move, pulling out until her body squeezed the head of my cock before I pushed back in. I moved slowly, savoring the slick feel of her around me. Her body was warm and so, so soft, and she felt so fucking good that I almost couldn't believe it was real. I wanted to take my time, to make this moment last as long as possible, but my body urged me to go faster. Harder.

"Oh, fuck...Tristan. Please...More..."

Her breathless words were all the encouragement I needed. Rising onto my elbows, I picked up the pace, thrusting deep inside of her until my balls were slapping against her and my heart was hammering in my chest. Luna moaned, her body arching beneath me, helping me go deeper still. I felt her tightening around me, like she was trying to pull me in, to make me a part of her.

And, oh fuck, I wanted that more than anything. To sink so deep inside of her, there was nothing but Luna.

But that thing inside me was still there, lurking in the shadows. I could feel it watching, waiting for the moment when I would lose control and let it take over. I tried to fight it, to keep myself in check, but it was too much. It was all too fucking much.

Luna's cries grew louder, more desperate. Sweat glistened on her skin and she tensed beneath me. I wanted to make her come, to give her the release she so desperately needed. And that focused me.

Ducking my head, I sucked one nipple into my mouth, running my tongue over the hard bud before nipping it with my teeth.

Luna bucked beneath me and cried out.

I lost control, my body moving on its own now with little direction from me. I thrust harder, deeper, faster. Luna trembled beneath me, the force of my cock pounding into her, shoving her body up on the mattress, but I couldn't stop. I needed this. I needed to feel her around me, to feel her surrender to me.

Luna threw her head back on the pillow, and my name left her lips on a cry. And then she came, her body convulsing beneath me, clenching my swollen cock with her orgasm. I thrust harder, my muscles shaking as the bottom of my spine tingled and my balls tightened.

With an animalistic cry, I joined her, my cock pulsing as I released inside of her. I didn't know if I was hurting her. I was too lost in the moment. Lost in the pleasure and the pain of not knowing where she ended and I began. And in that moment, I felt a strange sense of relief.

I was finally free.

When it was over, I collapsed on top of her, still shaking. I felt her heart pounding against my chest and her lungs fighting for breath, just as mine were.

With a moan of relief and regret, I pulled out and rolled off her.

We laid there in the dark, catching our breath, until I got up and went into the attached bathroom to get something to clean her off.

"I can do that myself if you'll untie me," she said when I came back with a towel. Leaving it on the bed, I pulled on my lounge pants and long-sleeved shirt. It would be hot, but I wasn't ready for her to see the horrors underneath. Not yet. I was already feeling too unbalanced by what had just happened. I didn't clean myself. I wanted to sleep with her cum coating my cock.

When I was dressed, I untied her ankles and then her wrists. Backing away, I gave her room to get up. "Thank you," she told me shyly. Then she gestured toward the bathroom. "Can I just...?"

"Of course."

I stared after her as she grabbed up the towel and headed to the bathroom, completely nonplussed by her nudity. My eyes fell to her lush ass, and I wished I'd had the forethought to turn on the light.

Once she was behind the closed door, my eyes fell to the rumpled blankets on my bed, unsure of what to do with her now. I'd promised her she could sleep in a real bed tonight, and that meant sleeping with me, as this bed was the only bed in the house. But I suddenly wanted her back in the cell. The cell was where she belonged. Where she was safe. I was too on edge, and I needed time to sort through everything that had happened.

Walking over to the window, I stared out into the darkness, trying to process not just what happened here tonight, but...everything. The night air was cool against my heated skin as it seeped through the old window, but I barely noticed.

Visions of Luna underneath me slammed around my head, casting light into the darkest corners of my soul. Lifting my hand, I put my fingers in my mouth. I could still taste her. I could still smell her on my skin. She was a part of me now. She was mine. And I wanted to keep her.

No. I wasn't thinking straight, because doing that would redefine my entire existence, and the weight of it left me feeling confused. Confined in a way I hadn't known since I was a child. I took a step back, rejecting the vision dancing around in my head. One of a life where someone was waiting at home for me. Someone who would smile at me when they saw me, the way Veda and Sera smiled at Luca and Enzo. Someone who cared about me.

Would I be able to care about Luna the same way? To... love her?

Love was an alien concept to me. I watched the way Luca acted with Veda. And Enzo with Sera. I didn't have those kinds of feelings. Yet, it was obvious I wasn't indifferent to Luna. Not at all. I felt a new crack in my carefully constructed armor every time I was around her.

But that was impossible. Sociopaths didn't feel emotions. Not the way everyone else did.

Perhaps this was nothing but a fleeting obsession. I felt a connection to Luna because of our shared traumas with Gino, and that was all it was.

I rubbed my temples, refusing to acknowledge the small, secret part of me that knew it was more. My interest in her may have started out as nothing but a reaction, a need to protect someone who couldn't protect themselves. But now it was more. Much, much more.

And that was dangerous. Not only for Luna. But for Luca and Enzo. And, mostly, for myself.

All I knew was that I wasn't ready to let her go.

CHAPTER 10

Luna

Tristan's face seemed softer in sleep, almost innocent if you ignored the hard set of his jaw and the lethal aura that clung to him even in slumber. But I knew that this glimpse of vulnerability was nothing but an illusion.

Or was this the real man underneath the cold façade?

I thought he would tie me up again when I came out of the bathroom, or send me back to the cell, and I knew he'd considered it. What happened here tonight had shaken him. Even I could see that. But after running his eyes over my naked body, he'd turned away, sitting on the side of the bed closest to the door. Grabbing my shirt off the floor, I put it on and crawled under the blankets on the opposite side. God, the mattress felt like heaven.

Holding very still, I tried to make myself as small and unobtrusive as possible.

Eventually, he laid down on top of the blankets on his side of the bed, as close to the edge as he could.

As I watched him lying there so stiffly, staring at the ceiling, something inside me gave a little. I almost felt bad for making him so uncomfortable in his own bed, but I wasn't about to offer to go back to the hard, cold floor in the cell.

I was starting to understand him a little better, though. Underneath the cold stares and unyielding demeanor—walls he'd built to protect himself from further pain—he was more damaged than any person I'd ever met. And I'd met some fucked-up people. We all had walls, though. Some were just higher than others.

He wasn't just a killing machine for Luca. He was a man. A man with a past as horrifying as the scars that marred his skin. I'd only seen a glimpse of them, but I knew they were there. Secrets Enzo had only touched on. I'd felt the rough texture of them against my breasts and stomach when he'd fucked me.

I wondered what it was like to live with such violence etched into your flesh? To relive all that pain every time you looked into a mirror?

The thought made my heart clench. A part of me longed to slide over to his side of the bed and hold him. But I knew he would never allow such compassion. Such intimacy.

Still, something between us had shifted tonight.

After an hour or so of tossing and turning, his breathing evened out, and he finally drifted off to sleep from what I could only imagine was pure exhaustion. I closed my eyes and tried to enjoy the feeling of the soft mattress cradling my sore bones, but after what seemed like only a few seconds, they snapped back open again. I must've dozed off for a bit, though, because Tristan had rolled closer to me. He was now on his stomach with his arms bent near his head. His face was turned away.

My eyes traveled along his strong arm, bent at the elbow with his hand shoved under the pillow. The sleeve was shoved up, revealing his bare forearm.

Taking a deep breath, I reached out a tentative hand and, ever so lightly, I brushed my fingertips along his scarred skin, tracing the ragged, ropey texture.

Tristan tensed at my touch, but didn't wake.

I knew I should stop before I woke him, but I couldn't. Even in the darkness, I could see the raised, jagged edges of old wounds. What had caused them? A knife? A cigarette? I drew in a ragged breath at the thought of someone being so evil they'd hurt a young boy this way, leaving such permanent reminders.

My fingers continued their feather-light exploration, tracing along the ridges and valleys of the scars. I wondered if he'd ever known a gentle touch before. From what Enzo told me, physical affection or comfort hadn't been part of Tristan's childhood. Just cruelty and pain.

My heart ached for the little boy who'd never had the chance to be a child. I wondered who he'd be if this hadn't happened to him. Or, for that matter, what kind of woman I'd be if I hadn't been thrown into the foster system and forced to use my body to appease my guardian so he wouldn't throw us out onto the street. Would we have still found each other?

Lost in thought, I almost didn't notice when Tristan's arm tensed under my fingertips. I froze, holding my breath, worried I'd woken him. But after a moment, he relaxed again, his breathing deep and even.

Letting out a quiet sigh of relief, I continued mapping the terrain of his arm. I traced along a particularly jagged scar near his elbow, feeling the ridge of toughened skin.

I only knew what Enzo had told me about what Tristan had been through. And honestly, I didn't know if I wanted to understand more. But I wanted to believe that underneath the violence, underneath the darkness, there was something more than a cold-blooded killer.

My fingers drifted down to his wrist, then the back of his hand. I softly outlined his knuckles. So strong, yet capable of surprising tenderness when he touched me.

These hands had squeezed the life from a man right in front of me, but they'd also carried me away and shielded me from harm, in his own fucked-up way.

I was playing with fire, I knew, touching him like this. If he woke up, he'd likely throw me back into the cell. Or worse. But I couldn't make myself stop. This was the first time I'd been able to touch him so freely, and I was going to take advantage of the opportunity while I could.

Continuing my exploration up his forearm, I kept my touch feather-light. His skin was warm, almost hot, beneath my fingertips. I could feel the coiled tension in his muscles, despite being relaxed in sleep. He was always on guard, ready to strike.

Suddenly he moved, rolling onto his side as his hand struck out, quick as a snake, and clamped around my wrist in a vise-like grip.

I cried out in pain and surprise.

His eyes flashed open and fixed on me with a predatory intensity that made my heart hammer in my chest. "What the fuck do you think you're doing?" he snarled, his voice low and dangerous.

I sputtered for an answer, but couldn't seem to say anything coherent. "I...I just..."

He yanked me closer, his eyes blazing. *"Don't touch me. Ever."* Then he released my wrist and rolled off the bed, putting distance between us by pacing to the other side of the room. There, he stopped, his fists clenched at his sides. His sharp, heavy breaths loud in the silence.

I shrank from him, pushing myself into a sitting position against the headboard and wrapping my arms around myself. "I'm sorry," I whispered.

Fear pooled in my stomach as he suddenly strode toward me, his face hard as granite and a calculating look in his eyes.

Grabbing my upper arm, he pulled me from the warm bed and half-walked, half-dragged me from the room, his fingers biting into my skin. I struggled feebly in his grip as he pulled me down the hall to the guest bedroom and the cell inside. He unlocked the door and threw me in, slamming it shut behind me. The clang of metal making me jump. I collapsed to the cold floor, shaking and fighting back tears as I pleaded with him. "Please, Tristan. I'm sorry. Don't leave me in here."

His eyes held mine for a moment longer, their icy depths unreadable. Then he turned on his heel and stalked from the room, leaving me alone in the cold, silent cell.

I stayed on the floor, my heart pounding against my ribcage like a trapped bird. The cold seeped into my bones, but it was nothing compared to the flash of betrayal in Tristan's eyes.

I wrapped the blanket around me as sobs wracked my body. I'd ruined the progress we'd made tonight. Now I was his prisoner again instead of his...what? Friend? Lover? I didn't even know.

I hugged myself tight, trying to ward off the cold and the unsettling thoughts swirling in my mind. But no matter how hard I tried to deny it, I couldn't ignore the fact that my feelings for Tristan were growing more complicated by the minute.

I should hate him. But I didn't. And I didn't know what to make of it. But this sure as hell wasn't a fairytale romance. This was a dance with danger. A dance that had just begun, and one I may never be free of.

The bedroom door suddenly locked with an ominous click, leaving me at the mercy of this dangerous and unpredictable man.

CHAPTER 11

Tristan

A black fog crept into the corners of my vision as I spiraled into the dark vortex of my memories. Spinning. Spinning. There was nowhere for me to go to escape. My pulse raced and I couldn't catch my breath.

This time, though, I wasn't alone in the darkness. There was someone new with me. Luna's big, blue eyes were everywhere I looked, filled with pain and confusion and sadness.

Please, Tristan. I'm sorry. Don't leave me in here.

Her voice had cracked with emotion, and something inside of me had broken in response. But I had to leave her there. I had to. I couldn't trust her, and she'd proven that tonight.

So I'd left her in my hell, my hands shaking as I locked the cell door. I needed to get out of there, away from her and the demons she'd resurrected with the innocent touch of her fingers on my arm.

Taking a deep breath, I tried to clear my mind of the chaos inside of it. Tried to shake off the memories. But it was too late. My fight-or-flight instinct had kicked in, and since I couldn't flee my demons, my natural reaction was to strike out.

But I couldn't hurt her.

Never her.

She was safer inside the cell. And I wouldn't be letting her out again. Not after tonight.

I dressed and gathered my weapons before leaving the house. Comforting darkness enveloped me as I walked away, each step taking me further from her pleading voice. My hands were still shaking, so I shoved them in my pockets, balling them into fists.

Getting into the SUV, I headed into the city.

The Russian I was watching last night would be at Luca's strip club tonight. I knew this because I'd overheard him making plans with a friend before I'd left his place at dawn. The kid had been causing trouble, stirring up shit he had no business being involved in. Luca decided he couldn't let him stay, not when he's only going to cause more problems for us. He wanted him taken out, and tonight I was more than happy to carry out that order. I needed something to pull me out of my head. I was a day early, but I didn't think Luca would care much, as long as the job got done.

I didn't remember driving to the club or parking the vehicle a few blocks away. The shadows seemed to cling to me as I moved through the back alleys, avoiding the well-lit streets. My boots crunched on broken glass and debris scattered on the pavement, and the sounds and smells of the city grounded me, keeping my demons at bay. Tonight, I would purge this darkness with blood and pain until the screams in my head went silent.

It wasn't long before I spotted my target walking up the street from the spillover parking lot. And he was alone. I slipped into the shadows, my nerves eerily calm as they always were when I was in these types of situations. My heart slowed to a steady rhythm, my breathing shallow, and my vision grew sharp as my instincts went on full alert. Silently, I followed him through the dark streets.

We approached the alley next to the club, and I pulled my knife from my back pants pocket. I was dressed to fight tonight in black BDU pants and a long-sleeved shirt, and my thick-soled boots made very little noise. He didn't even hear me until I was right up on him.

I was four steps away when he swung around, pulling a gun from inside his jacket and pointing it in my direction.

"You can't take weapons into the club," I informed him.

"What business is it of yours?" he demanded in a heavy Russian accent.

My lips pulled back in a feral grin. "Because my boss owns this place."

His eyes widened with fear a split second before they clouded over with resignation. "You're here for me."

I didn't bother to answer him. What was the point?

I saw the moment he decided to take me out first and launched myself at him. He didn't even have time to pull the trigger before I backed him up with a left hook to the jaw. Then I knocked the gun out of his hand.

But he was prepared.

Light glinted off the blade of the knife that appeared in his other hand. He came at me, slashing it wildly through the air. I easily dodged his clumsy attacks before grabbing his wrist and squeezing until he cried out, the knife clattering to the ground to join the gun. Still holding his wrist, I head-butted him, feeling bone and cartilage crunch under the impact. He howled in pain, hands flying to his broken nose.

I grabbed the kid by the front of his shirt and slammed him back against the brick wall of the alley before letting go again. He was dazed, blood streaming from his nose and down his chin.

"Please," he gasped, his fingers like talons as he tried to keep me away. "Don't do this."

I stared at him impassively, feeling nothing as I regarded his battered face. "It's nothing personal," I told him evenly. "I'm just following orders. And you should've stayed in New York."

His eyes widened in terror as I wrapped one hand around his throat. He struggled weakly, but already his movements were growing sluggish as I cut off his air supply. I watched as his face turned red, then purple. His eyes bulged and his mouth gaped like a fish out of water.

Only then did I slide my knife between his ribs, the sharp blade nicking bone before finding the space between his ribs, over and over, until we were both covered in his blood.

Just as his body went limp, I heard a noise at the end of the alley. I turned to see a couple of drunk guys stumbling past, likely on their way to blow their paychecks on Luca's dancers. Cursing under my breath, I let the kid drop bonelessly to the ground and stepped back into the shadows.

Pulling a burner phone out of my pocket, I dialed Milo's number. "I need you to get to the alley that runs alongside Luca's club," I told him when he answered. "As soon as possible."

"I'm already on my way."

I ended the call and destroyed the phone, tossing it into the nearby Dumpster as I passed it. I waited several beats before I left the alley and went back to my car, keeping my head down and staying out of the light so no one would see the shine of blood on my clothes.

Checking to make sure I hadn't been seen, I got back in the SUV and started to drive, the Russian already forgotten. I paid no attention to where I was going until I saw the gates leading onto Luca's property. The blood lust had subsided, as had the demons that demanded the sacrifice. Except for one.

Luna.

Now, an entirely different kind of lust was taking over. And if she was so interested in the scars that covered me, well, hell, maybe I'd just let her fucking see them.

A cold sweat broke out across my skin as I thought of undressing in front of Luna. Of letting her see me for what I was. And part of me wanted her to know me. All of me. Just like I now knew all of her.

My dick swelled at the memory of her wet heat pulsing around it.

I parked my car in the driveway and stepped out, my boots crunching on the gravel. The night air cooled my face, and I took a deep breath, the smell of blood and violence filling my nose.

Light spilled out from the windows of the house, casting shadows on the grass and driveway. I knew Luna was inside, waiting for me. Probably pacing my cell, waiting for me to come back so she could beg and plead with me to let her out. Or perhaps she would scream at me this time. Now that she'd had a taste of freedom, she'd want more. She didn't understand that she was safe in there. Didn't appreciate the peace I offered her.

I unlocked the front door and stepped inside, my heart beating a staccato rhythm in my chest. I'd make her fucking scream. But not in anger.

As I stalked to the back of the house where the bedrooms were located, the smell of sex lingered in the air, and I moaned aloud, knowing she was caught like a bird in a cage. Helpless. Unable to get away.

The bedroom door creaked as I opened it, and Luna's eyes widened in fear when she saw me. I could only imagine what I looked like in the soft light of the lamp.

I unlaced my boots and kicked them off. "You want to see them?" I asked her. "Do you want to see what your *father* did to me?" Grabbing the bottom of my shirt, I started lifting it up, turning at the last second so my back was to her. I'd save the best for last.

I heard her sharp intake of breath behind me, and I froze for just a second before I continued pulling off my bloody shirt.

Was it the blood? Or my scars that had her speechless?

I glanced over at the lamp on my nightstand. It seemed unnaturally bright. But I guess it didn't matter. Not now. Slowly, I turned around.

Luna stood in the middle of the cell. Her hair was disheveled, and her blue eyes were wide on my face. I lifted my chin in challenge, and she dropped them to my chest and arms, then lower, to my stomach, and over to my left hip where a wide, raised white scar curled toward my groin before disappearing beneath my pants. Her expression was hard to read as her eyes met mine.

"Do you like them?" I taunted. "Is this what you wanted to see, Luna?" I glanced down at myself, staring almost fondly at the horrific memories. "The round ones, they're from bullets. But the rest...I can still feel them, you know. Every single one. I can still feel them being carved into my body. Except for these." I ran my fingers over a neat, straight scar above my left pec. "These I didn't feel. See, I had to release it somewhere. The pain. The fear. The anger and frustration. It had to go somewhere. It couldn't stay inside of me anymore. I had to let it out, or I was going to combust from the inside out and there'd be nothing left of me but bloody pieces of meat. I had to let it out." I wanted her to understand. It was important to me that she understood.

"Tristan," she whispered.

My eyes flashed up to hers. They were filled with pity. I didn't want her fucking pity. "Hands," I ground out.

She approached me without hesitation and held her hands through the bars. Pulling the belt from my slacks, I used it to bind them together. Then I unlocked the door and stepped into the cell, the door clicking shut behind me. The smell of her fear was intoxicating.

"Who did you kill tonight?" she asked softly.

I met her eyes. "Whoever I'm ordered to. It doesn't matter." I moved to stand behind her, enjoying the way her shirt barely covered her ass. "Are you wearing anything beneath that shirt, Luna?"

She didn't answer.

Her midnight hair hung in wild waves just past her shoulder blades. I decided I preferred it like this when she slept, instead of captured in a braid the way she usually had it. I realized I'd forgotten to put hair bands in the bathroom for her before I brought her here, and I was glad.

With my blood-stained hands, I lifted the bottom of the shirt she wore until the rounded curves of her ass were on full display. I ran one fingertip along the crack between them, then cupped one cheek in my large hand and squeezed. I loved her skin, so soft and supple and pale against the darker tan of my hands. So flawless. Unlike my own. I loved all of her body, the curves and dips and grace of it.

I ran my palms over the outside of her hips and thighs as far down as I could reach before I came back up. Reaching around her, I shoved my hands under her shirt and cupped her breasts...

Her head fell back against my chest. Long, dark hair tickling my skin. My breath caught, and I froze, heart pounding hard, my eyes on her stunning profile. Her eyes were closed, and her lips were parted. I released my breath on a hiss, forcing myself to stay where I was.

When she realized I wasn't moving, her eyes fluttered open, and she quickly lifted her head. "I'm sorry," she whispered.

"It's okay," I told her. "It's okay." I wasn't sure who I was trying to convince more, her or me. With shaking hands, I shoved her shirt up as far as I could, then lifted it up and over her head and pushed it down her arms until it hit the bars.

Luna slowly lowered her head back to rest against me. This time, I was expecting it, and I was less reactive.

However, the sound I made was raw and desperate as I looked down at her breasts with their hard nipples jutting out over the soft curve of her stomach. From this angle, I couldn't see her pussy. But that was good, because I didn't think I'd be able to control myself if I could.

I touched her the way I always did, as if her body was mine to do with as I wished, running my hands up over her soft belly to heft the weight of her breasts in my hands, playing with her nipples with my thumbs.

"Tristan, I want to touch you."

My blood turned to ice at her words, and I shook my head, unable to speak. My hands tightened on her breasts.

"Please. Untie my hands. Let me touch you."

"I can't," I managed to get out past the tightness in my throat.

Luna yanked her arms down, trying to force her wrists from the belt.

"Stop it," I growled.

She did it again, harder this time. And again. And again. I could see the skin around her wrists turning red from the stiff leather.

"Stop it!" I wrapped my hands around her forearms, trying to hold her still.

"No," she snarled. "Fucking untie me." Even with me holding her arms, she managed to give them another good yank.

Panicked now that she was going to hurt herself, I grabbed her jaw and turned her face until she was looking at me. As angry as I was with her, I couldn't keep the strain from my voice when I asked, "Why are you doing this to yourself?"

She stared up at me defiantly and wet her lips with her tongue, making them glisten.

A low growl rumbled in my chest as I followed the movement. Luna's eyes flashed with defiance. Lowering my head, I took her mouth with mine, nipping at her full bottom lip until she opened for me and let me in.

The anger in her kiss was palpable, and I gripped her jaw so she couldn't pull away. My overwhelming need for her simmered just below the surface, threatening to boil over at any moment.

"You want to touch me, Luna?" I asked, my voice a low, dangerous rumble in her ear. "You want to feel my skin against yours? To know me, as I know you?" She didn't answer, her eyes flashing fire.

"You can't," I told her, my voice rough with the effort to hold back my own desire.

She yanked her arms down again, hard. "Fuck you."

What I couldn't say was I wanted her to touch me.

Fucking *hell*, I wanted her to touch me.

CHAPTER 12

Luna

My wrists burned where the leather of the belt cut into my skin, but I barely felt it as I pulled my arms down hard and fast through the bars until it caught. I felt the belt give a little, and I wriggled my hands around, trying to stretch it out more.

Tristan's breathing was fast and harsh, his scarred chest rising and falling against my naked back. "You're bleeding." His voice was strained. He tightened his grip on my forearms and rolled his hips, pressing his erection into my lower back.

I ignored the pain in my wrists as I fought with the belt. "Let me go." I spat the words out, not thinking. I just knew I was tired of having no control.

Tristan's grip on my arms tightened even more, and he leaned down to whisper in my ear. "You know I can't do that." His voice was low and rough, and it sent a shiver down my spine.

I closed my eyes and took a deep breath, trying to calm myself down, but something inside of me had had enough of this bullshit. "You can. You just won't."

"No," he agreed. "I won't."

I was his captive, and there was no escape. But that didn't mean I had to make it easy for him.

I struggled against the belt, trying to pull my arms free, but it was no use. Tristan ran his hand down my side, his fingers tracing the curve of my hip. "Why are you trying to hurt yourself?"

I glared at him over my shoulder, my eyes flashing with anger. "Because you're a monster, and I'm trying to get the hell away from you."

Tristan's expression darkened with something I couldn't read, and I quickly tore my eyes from his and faced forward again.

But he grabbed my chin, forcing me to look at him. "Say that again."

I swallowed hard, my heart racing as I stared into the cold darkness of his eyes. I knew I was playing with fire, but something inside of me wanted to get some kind of reaction from him. To make him *feel*, like I was feeling. "You're a monster."

His eyes narrowed, and he leaned in, his lips brushing gently against mine. A direct contrast to the fire now raging between us. "You have no fucking idea what I really am." Then he kissed me hard, his tongue forcing its way into my mouth. I tried to pull away, but he was too strong. The metal was icy cold against my heated skin as he pinned me to the bars, his heavy body pressing into mine from behind.

I moaned into his mouth, unable to stop myself. Despite everything, I couldn't deny the way my body responded to him. Something hot and wild coiled inside when he touched me, and I ached for him in spite of myself. He was a monster, but he was also the only person who had ever made me feel this alive. Unlike every other man I'd ever been with, I couldn't shut him out, much as I wanted to.

Tristan pulled away, his breathing ragged. "Besides, you're lying. You don't want to be free. Not really. You want me as much as I want you."

"No," I lied between clenched teeth. I tried to deny it, but again, my body betrayed me. I was wet and aching for him, and I hated myself for it.

His warm breath tickled the outer shell of my ear as he ran his hand down my stomach, his fingers slipping between my legs. "Fuck, Luna. You're so fucking wet for me already."

I bit my lip, trying to hold back a moan as he stroked me. "Please," I whispered, not even sure what I was asking for.

He rolled his hips, and I felt his hard length through his pants. "I want you to beg me."

I shook my head, trying to clear the fog from my brain. "No, I won't."

"Yes, you will." He slid his hands down my body and gripped my hips, pulling them back until I had no choice but to step back and bend over, my arms stretched taut and the belt cutting into my aching wrists. "You're going to beg me to fuck you."

I closed my eyes, trying to block out the sound of his voice, but it was no use. There was no escape. I was at his mercy, and he was right.

I fucking loved it.

Tristan leaned over me and dropped kisses down my spine. I moaned and pushed my ass against him, trying to get closer. There was a heavy ache in my lower stomach, and I could feel his erection pressing against me. I wanted him inside me.

He pulled away and slid his hand between us, his fingers finding my clit from behind. He stroked me slowly, teasing me, until I moaned and writhed against him.

His thumb slid inside of me, and his breathing picked up. "You're so fucking tight." He thrust it in and out, his fingers mimicking the movement on my clit, and I bucked my hips as tension coiled low in my stomach, pressure building inside of me. Fuck, I was going to come. I didn't want to, but I couldn't stop myself.

Tristan suddenly pulled his hand away, and I heard the sound of his zipper a moment before his erection sprang free and hit my ass. He grabbed my hips and pulled me close again, the thick head of his cock pressing against my entrance. "Beg me," he growled. "Tell me you want me."

I shook my head, trying to hold on to my last shred of dignity. "No."

Kicking my feet farther apart, his fingers found my clit again, and he stroked me in fast circles. I was so, so wet. And it felt so fucking good.

"Beg me," he growled again.

I closed my eyes and bit down, trying to steady myself. I didn't want to give him the satisfaction of knowing he had broken me.

But I couldn't hold out any longer. I was on the edge, and I needed him to push me over. "Please," I whispered, my voice shaking. "Fuck me."

Without another word, he pushed inside me, his thick cock filling me completely. I cried out and dropped my head forward so my hair hid my shame, my entire body trembling with pleasure and the need to come. He pulled out and thrust again, harder this time, and I cried out again, my nails digging into the bars of the cell.

"Harder," I hissed, my voice barely above a whisper. "Fuck me harder."

But he heard me. With a growl, he pounded into me with renewed force, his hips slapping against my ass with each brutal stroke. The pain and pleasure of our violent lovemaking left me gasping and panting, my body responding to his every command until I came so hard, my knees gave way and only his hands on my hips kept me upright.

He groaned and thrust hard one last time, his cock pulsing inside me as he collapsed over my back, his breathing ragged and his heart pounding in time with mine.

Tears filled my eyes. I'd just had angry, almost violent sex with my captor, and I'd loved every fucking minute of it.

Still inside of me, I shivered as his lips pressed against my sensitive skin. "You're mine," he whispered.

I opened my mouth, but I couldn't bring myself to deny it.

Gently now, he lifted his weight from me and pulled out. Goosebumps rose on my skin as the cool air dried the sweat from my skin. I stepped closer to the bars and straightened, noticing for the first time how my wrists screamed with pain. Blood dripped from them onto the hard floor, and his cum ran down my inner thighs.

Tristan cursed softly and left the cell, locking me in again before he undid the belt from around my wrists. "Jesus, Luna."

When his dark eyes met mine, I was overwhelmed with emotion as a raw truth slammed into me. I was falling for my captor, and I didn't know what to do.

Hot tears overflowed and slid down my cheeks.

Tristan reached through the bars and took my face between his bloody hands, wiping them away with his thumbs. Then he kissed me again, his lips soft and gentle like I was something precious. Breakable. "You're mine," he repeated, his deep voice barely audible, before he kissed me again.

I closed my eyes and let myself sink into the kiss, trying to ignore the voice in the back of my head that screamed I was getting in too deep. But I didn't know how to get out.

And hell, maybe I didn't want to. What was waiting for me if I did? Gino? Was he even looking for me? Did he care that I was gone? "Is Gino looking for me?" I asked when he ended the kiss.

He still held my face in his hands, our faces only inches apart.

"Yes."

Icy fear cooled my blood. I remembered the gun my father held to my head, and yeah, maybe being here wasn't so bad for the time being. It would be nice to get out of this fucking cell, though.

Tristan released me, and I pulled my shirt back on, wincing as the fabric brushed against my raw wrists. When I lifted my head again, Tristan was walking from the room, his shirt hanging from his hand. "Where are you going?"

He didn't answer.

I sighed and went into the bathroom and started the shower. The soap and water burned my wrists like hell as I washed them, and the water ran pink and red. When I got out, I wrapped the towel around myself and looked for some bandages or something, but there was nothing. So, I used toilet paper.

Dressed in baggy black sweats and a T-shirt, I went back out into the cell. The girl on the walls mocked me. I missed that girl. She was far from innocent, but she got to sleep in a real bed and even got to go outside and to parties sometimes.

After what felt like an eternity, the door opened, and he came back into the room. He was dressed comfortably again, and he was holding a first aid kit in one hand and a bottle of something in the other. The blood was gone from his hands and face and his hair was wet.

Unlocking the cell, he stepped inside and gestured for me to join him in the bathroom. "Let me see your wrists," he ordered quietly.

I held them over the sink, and Tristan unwrapped my makeshift bandages. Then he gently cleaned my injuries, his touch surprisingly gentle. I winced as he poured peroxide over them, but I didn't pull away.

When they were clean, he bandaged my wrists again with real gauze this time. With a finger under my chin, he lifted my face to his until I was forced to meet his hard gaze. "Don't do that again."

I dropped my eyes. I wouldn't make a promise I didn't know that I'd be able to keep.

Releasing me, he took a step back. "I'm tired," he said. "It's been a long night."

I closed my eyes, the thought of sleeping on that hard floor almost too much.

"Bring what you want with you."

Wait. What?

He left me standing in the bathroom. I watched him walk out of the cell, leaving the door wide open. The bedroom door too.

Unplugging my new cell phone, I hurried out after him. But in the hallway, I paused, not sure which way to go.

After what had happened earlier, I didn't think he'd want me anywhere near him unless my hands were bound.

"Are you coming?"

My head whipped around, and I found him standing in the doorway to his room.

"Yeah," I told him. "Yes. I'm coming."

He closed the door behind me and waited for me to use the bathroom and get into bed before he turned off the light and joined me, laying on top of the comforter like he had earlier. "Do I need to tie your hands?"

"No. Absolutely not."

"Good." Rolling over onto his side, he put his back to me.

Slipping under the covers, I pulled them up to my chin and closed my eyes.

I woke to the sound of Tristan's voice, low and rough, as he spoke on the phone in Italian. I laid still, trying to make out what he was saying, but my wrists were throbbing, and I had to pee. Plus, I knew very little Italian. Only what I'd picked up playing poker at the club.

Slowly, I opened my eyes to find him watching me from the chair across the room, showered and fully dressed in one of his expensive suits.

Throwing off the blankets, I hurried into the bathroom. There was an extra toothbrush laying by the sink, still in its wrapper.

When I came back out, bladder relieved, face washed, teeth brushed, and hair wrestled into something that no longer resembled a bird's nest, I found him waiting for me. "What is it?" Something was wrong. I could feel it, even though his expression revealed nothing.

He rose from the chair, sliding his phone into the inside pocket of his coat. There was a gun strapped to his side. When he reached me, he took my face in his hands and kissed me hard, his lips moving on mine like he'd never kiss me again.

Still holding my face, he pulled away and pressed his forehead to mine. "Luna," he whispered, his voice hoarse. "You shouldn't be here."

I went to reach for him and stopped. My heart began to pound as a surge of panic filled me. "What do you mean?"

"You should go," he said, his voice barely above a whisper. "I should let you go."

CHAPTER 13

Tristan

"What? Wait. Wait!" she yelled.

I stopped, but didn't turn around. Just stared straight ahead. Because I was afraid if I looked at her, I'd throw her back in the cell and never let her out again. Just so I could keep her forever.

It was selfish of me. Keeping her had never been my intention. Although, honestly, I'd never really thought much about what I would do with her once I had her here. I only knew I *wanted* her. And Gino couldn't have her anymore.

As if she could read my mind, she asked, "What about Gino?"

I was giving her the chance to run. Why wasn't she taking it?

"What about Gino?" she repeated louder, a hint of desperation seeping into her voice.

Gino. My lips pulled back as I bared my teeth. In all of this...*this shit*—I didn't even know what to call it—between us, I'd set aside my plans for him. But she was right. If I let her go, he'd find her. Of that, I was certain.

"I'll take care of Gino," I said, my voice a low rumble, betraying none of the turmoil churning inside me. "You won't need to worry about him anymore." It was safer this way, to send her away. These strange, unsettling emotions she stirred inside of me were fucking with my head.

She was silent for a long moment. "What are you going to do, Tristan?"

"Whatever I have to." *To keep you safe. To put myself back together.*

"You told me..." Her voice broke, a small crack in her otherwise carefully composed façade. But she didn't fool me. I could see it all. The confusion, the pain, the inexplicable pull she felt toward something as dangerous and unpredictable as me, just as I was drawn toward her. Every instinct I had screamed at me to pull her into my arms, to protect her, to claim her.

That was exactly the problem, though, wasn't it? Luna was becoming more than a responsibility, more than someone weaker than myself I'd only wanted to protect. She'd become an obsession. And a dangerous one at that.

No, it was more than that. Without even trying, she was changing me. I didn't know who I fucking was anymore. My identity, my entire sense of self, it was all unraveling before my eyes. Everything I thought I knew about myself was shifting, morphing into something I didn't recognize.

But that wasn't right. I didn't...*feel* things. Emotions didn't rule my actions. Logic and instinct did. That's what made me good at my job. It's how I survived. It's what Luca and Enzo depended on when the only thing stopping a bullet from hitting them was me.

And yet, I felt something for her. Something other than curiosity and lust. There was an ache deep in my chest whenever I looked at her. A flicker of amusement when she dared to stand up to me, and frustration when she wouldn't listen. Even anger, at times. Things I hadn't felt since I was a very young child. Just flashes, but still, they were there.

I'd forgotten how distracting emotions were.

"You're just going to let me go? After everything you've done? Everything *we've* done. Just like that?" There was an edge to her voice now, a challenge. Luna was not the kind of woman to be discarded easily, and she knew it. She was strong, resilient, beautiful, and right now, she was calling me out.

I raised my eyes, allowing myself a glimpse of this chaotic force I'd brought into my life, not understanding how much damage she'd cause. Her eyes, a stormy mixture of fear and something that looked dangerously like hope, met mine. And in that moment, every wall I'd built, every rule I'd set for myself, threatened to crumble.

I took a step back, putting physical distance between us. "Yes," I said, the word bitter in my mouth. "It's safer for you to be away from me."

Her laugh was hollow, devoid of humor. "Safe? There's nothing safe about this world, Tristan. Not with men like my...Gino." She paused, her eyes running over me. "Men like you."

I closed my eyes, her sharp words stabbing something deep inside of me.

She came closer, getting into my personal space, but I didn't back down this time. "Why did you bring me here at all? Why put me through all of this if you're just going to throw me back out there?" She swung her arm toward the window.

The question hung in the air, heavy and unanswerable. Why, indeed.

"I don't know," I finally admitted. It was a confession she'd heard before, a tiny surrender to the confusion and fear she stirred within me.

Her blue eyes searched mine, looking for something more, something deeper. Her scent wrapped around me like a seductive shroud. "I think you do know," she said softly. "But you're too much of a coward to admit it."

A coward? At one time, that would've been laughable. And yet, at this moment, it was undeniably true. I was afraid to examine these strange behaviors I was exhibiting. Afraid of what I'd find there. Terrified that if I released them, I wouldn't be able to handle the surge of emotions I'd kept buried all these years.

Only one thing was more terrifying to me: that there would be nothing inside of me. Nothing but this cold, empty darkness.

I turned away, unable to face her. I didn't want to see the hurt I was inflicting. It was better this way. Feelings were a liability, a weakness. In my world, weaknesses got you killed. I had survived this long by being cold, unfeeling, a machine made of flesh and blood. But Luna, she threatened all of that with her warmth, her compassion, her quiet strength that had somehow found its way through the cracks in my armor.

I needed to let her go for my own sanity. But the thought of losing her, of letting her walk out of this room, out of my life, leaving me with nothing but that dark, empty void she had once filled...

It was unimaginable to me.

"What are you going to do, Tristan?" Her voice was barely above a whisper, but it echoed in the cavernous, empty spaces of my heart.

"I don't know," I said again, this time with a different edge to my voice. I realized I was telling the truth, and it was the beginning of something dangerous. Something uncontrollable.

I didn't *want* to let her go.

But would I be willing to risk everything to have her in my life? And if she knew what was really inside me, whatever that may be, would she still want me?

I had to tell her the truth. "I can't be what you need," I said, the words tasting like ash in my mouth. "Whatever you think I am, Luna. I'm not that. I can't pretend otherwise. Not even for you."

She came around to stand in front of me again, forcing me to look at her. "Maybe I don't need you to be anything other than who you are," she replied softly, a hint of defiance flashing in her eyes.

I stood there, frozen, as her words washed over me.

Mine.

The thought took root in my mind before I could stop it.

No. I clenched my jaw. This was dangerous territory I was wandering into. She couldn't mean it. Not after everything I'd done. Everything I'd do in the future. "And if I'm nothing but what you see in front of you?"

"I don't believe that."

"Then you're a fool."

And yet, the certainty in her eyes gave me pause. She wasn't afraid of me, not like she should be. Like any sane person would be. Luna looked at me like there was something worth saving underneath the horrific exterior.

And I almost believed her when she looked at me like that.

I raked a hand through my hair in frustration. I couldn't let my guard down. I couldn't let her in. My life didn't allow for softness or light. I lived in the darkness, and if I let her get too close, that darkness would swallow her whole.

"Tristan." Her voice was quiet, but insistent. Reluctantly, I met her gaze again. "It's okay to feel something real every once in a while. Even for someone like you."

I stared at her perfect face. "I don't know how." The words tore from my throat. "This is what I am, Luna. What I've always been."

She stepped closer, her hand coming up to touch my chest. I flinched before she could make contact, and her hand dropped back down to her side. She gave me a little smile of reassurance, but there was hurt in her eyes.

"Not what you've always been," she said. "You were forced to become what you are. Not born that way. And maybe you've forgotten what real emotions are, but they're still in there." Catching my eyes with hers, she forced me to see the truth on her face. "They're in there because I see them whenever you look at me. And I feel them in your kiss and in your touch. I feel *you*, Tristan."

My breath caught in my throat. I wanted to argue, to tell her she was imagining things. It was only my body's physical need she felt. "Luna..." I whispered her name like a prayer, still unsure what I was even asking for. Permission? Absolution? For her to save me from myself?

Before I could overthink it, I took her face in my hands, my mouth finding hers in a desperate need to connect with her in a way I understood. She melted into me, her lips soft and pliant under mine. I kissed her deeply, hungrily, like I was dying of thirst and only she could sustain me.

When we finally broke apart, breathless, her eyes searched mine, looking for answers I couldn't give her. "I don't know what any of this means," I admitted.

"Neither do I." She sounded as surprised as I was.

I stood there, caught in the web of her stare and unable to look away. For once, I had no idea what to do next.

Luna reached up slowly, giving me time to pull away if I wanted. When I didn't, her fingertips came to rest lightly against my cheek, then her entire palm. I swallowed hard as every muscle in my body stiffened, but I leaned into her touch, allowing myself this tiny moment of vulnerability. Her skin was soft and warm and felt foreign against my clenched jaw. After only a few seconds, I pulled away, unable to bear it anymore.

She accepted my rejection this time without comment. "What do you want, Tristan?" she asked.

I frowned at the offhand question. "What do I want?"

"Forget everything else for a second. Your job. Your past. Gino. If you could have something just for you, what would it be?"

I searched her face, confused. No one had ever asked me such a question before. I'd always done what was expected of me, what was necessary. What I'd been created for. What I'd wanted had never mattered. But the answer, when it came, was simple. "You." The word was ripped from some deep, hidden part of me. But it was the truth. I wanted her in a way I'd never wanted anything.

"Do you want me locked in your cell?"

I cocked my head, wondering what she was getting at. It was the safest place for her. I thought of her living a free life like the one she'd had before she lost the bet to Gino, and a red haze covered my vision. In my mind, I saw her going back to work, taking off her clothes for other men, letting them touch her in the private room in the back. "You're not going back to the club."

As if she heard the thoughts racing through my head, she held her hands up, palms out in a placating gesture. "I'm not going anywhere. I'm right here."

My heart stuttered and then slowed.

"But a moment ago, you were telling me I should leave."

"So, why are you still here?"

She lifted her chin. "I don't know, honestly."

My teeth began to ache, and I realized I was clenching my jaw again. She was talking in circles. I didn't understand. "What the fuck are you trying to accomplish here, Luna?"

"I'm just trying to understand you."

"Maybe you shouldn't do that."

I was a ruthless killer—cold, calculating, and dangerous. This world was all I'd ever known. What good could possibly come from delving deeper into the twisted inner workings of my mind?

"I'm not a good man, Luna," I pointed out what she already knew. "The things I've done..." I trailed off as visions of the past flashed through my mind. Broken bodies and lifeless eyes staring up at me. Cries for mercy falling on deaf ears. "You don't want to know me. Not really."

She watched me carefully, considering my words. "I'm not afraid of your past, Tristan. We all have skeletons in our closet."

I let out a harsh laugh. "Some more than others, *bambolina.*" Little doll. It was an apt name for her. My little doll in her cage.

Luna stepped closer, her eyes searching mine intently. "I know you think you're a monster. But I don't believe that."

I shook my head, astounded by her naivety. "Then, again, you're a fool." How could she not see the beast that lurked beneath the surface? The thing that lived inside me, that danced in the blood of the people I killed?

"Then tell me," Luna challenged. "Make me understand."

I raked a hand through my hair in frustration. Where could I even begin? The horrors of my childhood under Gino's sadistic hand? My soul-shattering first kill at the age of twenty-two? I sobered. Should I tell her about that one? Probably not while she was within reach of objects she could use as weapons.

The blood on my hands could fill an ocean.

"Please, Tristan," Luna pleaded gently. "Let me in."

I narrowed my eyes, becoming suspicious of her motives. What the hell was she doing? She'd done nothing but beg me to release her, denied her need for me over and over even though her body told me a different story, and now suddenly she wanted to stay? I'd spent my entire life building walls to keep everyone else out. No one had ever tried to scale them before. No one had ever wanted to truly know the monster caged within.

Until now.

I studied her, searching for any sign of deceit, and found nothing. If I let her in, allowed her to peer into the barren, twisted landscape of my soul, she would never look at me the same again. Instead, revulsion and fear would fill those striking blue eyes every time she looked at me.

But if I shut her out completely, I risked losing her. Not physically. I could keep her locked in that cell forever if I chose to. No one would fucking stop me. But still, I would lose her. Eventually. And then she would truly be like a doll that lived and breathed, but didn't feel, didn't live. She would sit in that cell just waiting to die.

She would become like me.

The thought sent an unexpected spike of panic through me. Swallowing hard, I tried to make sense of the mess inside my head. What the fuck was I supposed to tell her? What did she want to hear? Should I tell her of my childhood, of the cruelty I'd endured at her father's hands? Of how I'd learned cruelty myself, wielded it like a weapon to survive? Should I tell her how my first kill had numbed me, severing me from my humanity? How violence became my sole purpose, the only thing I was good at?

No. I couldn't tell her any of that. "I need to go take care of something, and I need you to go back to the cell while I do."

She stared up at me with tears in her eyes. "Tristan, don't keep locking me out."

"Do I need to drag you there?"

She drew back, blinking away the emotions as she composed herself. "No."

"Good."

With one last searching look, she grabbed her phone and walked out of my room and back to hers.

"Are you hungry?" I asked her once she was secured in the cell. "Do you need anything before I go?"

"How long will you be gone?"

"Not long."

She took a deep breath as she glanced around the cell. "Some coffee? With cream and sugar? And maybe some water? I'm not really hungry."

I thought about making her something anyway, but what I had to do shouldn't take more than a few hours. With a nod, I left the room to get her drinks, taking the time to clear my head. When I came back, I slid them along the floor through the bars.

"Tristan?"

"Yes?"

She stared at me for a long time, but then she just shook her head and looked away. "Nothing. Never mind."

The only thing I heard in her voice was...hopelessness.

CHAPTER 14

Tristan

I slowly opened my eyes, wincing at the pounding in my head. The world around me spun and my stomach lurched. I swallowed hard as I tried to take in my surroundings. I was in an unfamiliar room, lying on my back on a black leather couch. It was dark, lit only by a dim overhead light, but I could make out white walls and a cement floor. The air was damp and cold, and something was scratching inside the wall behind me. The sound was abnormally loud in the silent room.

The last thing I remembered was leaving the drop I'd made for Luca before lunch. How the fuck did I get here?

I looked down at myself. My suit jacket was unbuttoned, revealing my black dress shirt. My gun was gone, as was my knife. I patted my pants pocket. My phone wasn't there either, though that wasn't really a surprise. Lifting the sides of my jacket, I noticed the corner of something sticking out of the inside pocket. Pulling it out, I stared at the photo of Luna and her brother.

My lungs seized in my chest as the day's events came rushing back. I'd made the drop because Luca and Enzo were meeting with the other mafia bosses a few hours away. As a long-time capo, Gino was required to attend, so Luca thought it would be better if I wasn't there and sent me to meet his contact with the cartel, an old friend of Luca's who posed little risk. Before going back to the house, and knowing Luna's father would be occupied elsewhere, I went to Gino's. Our world was built on fragile alliances and power plays, and Gino was about to make one against Luca. We all knew it. I thought I would look around a bit and see what I could find, and while I was there, I'd grab anything I might have missed the first time for Luna before.

Gino's cars were gone from the driveway, but I parked a block away, just in case. As always, sneaking onto the grounds was easy. Squatting down behind a clump of brush at the edge of the front yard, I watched the house. No one came or went other than a guard out front. It appeared deserted.

Still, I used caution as I made my way to the back of the house where Luna's room was located. It was risky coming here in the middle of the day, but no riskier than at night when Gino and his men were home. I knew for a fact he only had a few security cameras, and I avoided them easily as I made my way to the back of the house and snuck into Luna's room through the window.

I found her old cell phone in the nightstand drawer and smashed it on the floor, tossing the pieces into the trashcan in the bathroom. I was sure Gino would use it to track her if I took it with me. Underneath it was the picture of Luna and her brother she'd mentioned when I'd brought her clothes to her. She was young in the photo, maybe nine. She stood next to her younger brother, one arm thrown over his shoulders. They were both grinning with the innocence of children who hadn't been thrown out into the world yet. It was probably taken right before their mother had died. Staring down at her sweet face, I realized this was what I'd come for. It would make her happy to have it back. I tucked it into the inside pocket of my suit jacket.

I made one last sweep of the room and went to the window. My phone vibrated in my pocket, and I paused to respond to Luca so I could let him know the drop had gone down without any issues, then I dropped it back into my pants pocket. One leg was out of the window, when suddenly a wet cloth was pressed to my face, and I breathed in the sickly-sweet smell of chemicals. I froze as strong arms tightened around me, trapping my arms. I tried not to breathe. I tried to fight back. But the shock of someone's arms around me had locked my muscles down in terror. The last thing I remembered was hearing Gino's voice giving orders, and then there was nothing but darkness.

He wasn't at the meeting with Luca. He'd been waiting.

For me.

Taking stock of my body, I didn't find any injuries, so I slid off the couch on shaky legs and crept slowly towards the door. I paused with my hand on the knob, straining to hear any sounds on the other side. Silence. Holding my breath, I tried the knob. It was locked.

I started to make my way around the room, looking for any other way out. There were no windows. Nothing I could use as a weapon. The only furniture was the couch I'd been lying on.

Staggering over to it, I flipped it over, looking for something I could use to pick the lock on the door. Tearing the protective fabric away, I studied the coiled springs. I didn't think about what would happen to me if I was still here when he returned. If I knew Gino, and I did, it wouldn't be a quick death. Especially not for me. I needed to get out of here.

But I wasn't fast enough.

The spring I was working on was just starting to loosen when I heard a key in the lock. Straightening, I spun around as four of Gino's men preceded him into the room.

He was dressed in black slacks and a pullover black shirt, the sleeves pushed up to reveal his forearms. In one hand, he held a whip. In the other, he held my knife. His eyes traveled over me slowly, with too much familiarity, before coming back to my face. "Hello, Tristan."

And with those two simple words, my blood froze in my veins as I was transported back, back, back to a room much like this one. I shook my head violently as screams filled my ears, but I couldn't tell if they were coming from me or just the demons in my head. I wasn't that child anymore. This wasn't that room.

Yet, I couldn't move as two of his men walked on either side of me and swiftly righted the couch, then joined the other two as they wrestled me down and stripped off my clothes.

The picture fell onto the floor. I couldn't take my eyes from it as the four men forced me to the back wall and chained my wrists to metal hooks on the ceiling. It was the only thing keeping me the slightest bit sane.

Until Gino walked over and picked up the photo.

I screamed and cursed at him to leave it alone, my fractured mind somehow associating Luna to the photo of her.

He didn't smile as he stared down at the children he'd given up. "She's beautiful, isn't she? Just like her mother."

"She's not yours," I snarled.

Dropping the picture back onto the floor, he stepped on it as he came over to me. Grabbing a fistful of my hair, he wrenched my head back. I stared down at him. In my mind, his eyes were glowing red, like the demon he was. "Where is my daughter, Tristan?"

I couldn't breathe, couldn't get enough air and my heart pounded in my ears so loud I could barely hear him. "Don't *touch* me," I growled.

He smiled at me then. "Oh, I'll do whatever the fuck I want to you. Just like always." The cold blade of my knife scraped down my chest to my cock. He rested the edge at the base. "And you'll like it."

I bared my teeth at him, even as I broke out into a cold sweat.

"You've always liked it. If you didn't, you wouldn't do things to get my attention, would you?" Knife still at my cock, he let go of my hair and ran his other hand over a few of the scars he'd left on me. My skin crawled beneath his rough palm, and my muscles went rigid.

He continued to taunt me, touching me everywhere—my chest, my stomach, my cock. "Where's my daughter, Tristan?"

"Fuck you!"

"Is that what you want? Because we can do that. I've got four men here who can bend you over the back of that couch." Reaching down, he gave my balls a squeeze. "You took my Luna away from me. I know you did. So you owe me."

I threw my head forward, smashing my forehead into his nose. The demon who haunted my nightmares cursed loudly as he stepped back out of range and covered his face protectively. "You son of a bitch!"

I thrashed against the chains as he pulled the whip from his back pocket and brought it back, but made no sound as the thick leather set my skin on fire. With so much scar tissue already, I barely felt it. Or maybe it was just because my mind had snapped and I was floating above my body, watching the scene act out from somewhere else. I wasn't dead. I could see my naked body twisting violently against the constraints that held it, could hear the animalistic screams torn from my throat as they tried to contain the monster they'd unleashed.

He was fucking hard. I could see the outline of his dick. And I knew what was coming next.

Like rushing through a bright tunnel, I was suddenly back in my body as a rough cord of rope was wrapped around my throat.

No. Noooo!!

One of the hooks came out of the ceiling, freeing my hand, and everything went red.

I reacted on instinct, driving my elbow into the gut of the fucker with the rope and grabbing the chain wrapped around my other wrist. A few seconds later, I'm not even sure how, both hands were free.

An inhuman scream filled the small room, echoing in my ears. Mine? Or one of theirs?

I lashed out with my fists, hitting flesh and breaking bones. Shots fired and there was a gun in my hand. Where did it come from? It didn't matter. I swung it around wildly, shooting at anything that moved.

Then suddenly, there was silence, and it was so loud it rang in my ears. Four bodies were bleeding out on the floor. The door to the room was open.

Gino was nowhere to be found.

My legs gave out, and I fell to the floor, landing half on top of one of the bodies. On my hands and knees, I crawled over to my clothes, my breath sawing in and out of my lungs and my heart racing. The only thought in my head was to escape.

One of my hands hit the picture, sending it sliding across the floor. I followed it, crawling awkwardly on one arm, my clothes in the other. When I reached it, it was so slippery I had a hard time picking it up.

The scratching noise started up again in the wall.

Forcing myself to my feet, I stumbled out of the room. There were stairs I somehow made it up, and then a long hallway to the left. To the right was a door. After a few tries, I got it open and then I was outside.

It was dark, but I could see well enough to know I was still at Gino's. My legs started to move, jogging across the yard to the tree line. Once I was under cover, I pulled on my slacks.

Next thing I knew, I was in the SUV, and it was running. One foot was on the gas and headlights were blinding me as voices threatened me, shouting in my ears.

Home.

I just needed to get home, where it couldn't hurt me.

CHAPTER 15

Luna

Something broke through my dreams. A noise. Nothing more than the scuff of a shoe, maybe. Sighing deeply, I tried to find a comfortable position on the hard floor. I couldn't have been sleeping very long, because my hip bone didn't hurt. My stomach growled. I'd had a hard time falling asleep, and I wasn't ready to wake up yet, and now lingered somewhere between sleep and consciousness, convinced I must've dreamed of the noise.

There it was again.

I pried my eyes open and found myself staring at the cream-colored wall at the back of my cell. At first, I stayed very still, listening for whatever had made the noise to do it again. While I waited, I prayed to any entity that happened to be listening that it wasn't a mouse. Or a rat. God, please no. Not a rat.

I nearly jumped out of my skin when I heard a soft moan and the clank of metal. Flipping over onto my back, I sat up, my eyes flying around the cell until they found the source.

Tristan sat in the opposite corner of the cell with his back against the corner where the bars met the wall, as far from the door as he could get. One leg was bent, and the other was straight out in front of him. He was wearing the suit he left in, but his shirt was balled up on the floor next to him and he was barefoot. Crumpled up wads of paper were scattered around him and there was a pad and pencil on the floor. The key to his car was by his foot.

His torso was covered in blood.

"Tristan?" I stumbled to my feet, shoving my hair out of my face, and hurried over to him. "What happened? Are you hurt?" I dropped down as close to him as I dared, wincing at the pain when my knees hit the hard floor. Without thinking, I reached out to touch him, pulling my hands back just in time. His chest and stomach were covered with cuts and bruises, and there were a few long welts. "Tristan? Tristan!"

His obsidian eyes stared straight ahead. He didn't seem to see me kneeling in front of him or hear me calling his name. I stuck my face right in front of his, and my breath caught in my throat. "Tristan?" I whispered. But he wasn't there. He wasn't with me. His eyes were cold. Dead. There was nothing there. *He* wasn't there.

I wasn't sure how much blood he'd lost. He was a little pale, but I didn't know if that was from his injuries or from whatever had happened to him.

"What should I do?" I asked him aloud. "Tell me what to do!"

He didn't move. Didn't respond in any way.

"Phone. I need a phone." I could call Enzo, or Luca, even. They could help me. Dropping my eyes to his pants, I looked for the telltale shape of a cell phone in his pockets.

And that's when I saw the knife in his hand. There was blood on the blade. "Oh, my god."

He'd done this to himself.

Wrapping my hand around the dull edge of the metal, I carefully wiggled the knife out of his grip and slid it across the floor, away from us. He didn't have his phone. Not unless he was sitting on it. Jumping to my feet, I ran into the bathroom and got mine from the sink where I was charging it and returned to Tristan. Sitting on my heels, I tapped the screen with a shaking finger, looking for the number Enzo had given me in case of emergency.

I hit the green call button. He answered on the first ring. "Luna? What's going on?"

"Enzo?"

There was a brief pause. "What's wrong?"

"It's Tristan. He's in the cell with me," I told him. "He's bleeding. He cut himself all up and he's not responding to me." My throat tightened on a sob.

"What happened? Luna?" he said when I didn't answer. "What the fuck happened?"

"I don't know," I finally choked out. "I don't know. He's been gone all day, and when I woke up, he was here. What should I do?"

I heard the wind over our connection, and then the slamming of car doors. "Where's the key to the cell?"

"I don't know. I don't know. I can't touch him!"

"Okay. Okay. Calm down. How bad did he cut himself?"

Wiping my eyes with the back of my free hand, I looked over his bare chest, stomach, and arms. "Um. I don't know. Not bad? I don't think. But, he's not talking. He's just staring straight ahead, like...like...he's not even here. I don't know what happened. I don't know where he is. I can't get through to him."

"Okay. Don't worry about that right now. Find something to press on any of those wounds that look bad. We're on our way."

I looked at Tristan's face. I didn't know where his mind was right now, and I had no idea how he'd react if I got too near him. "How am I supposed to do that? What if he freaks out on me?"

"Just do it, Luna. It'll be okay. Don't touch him with your bare hands."

"Okay." Grabbing Tristan's shirt off the floor, I wadded it up, hesitating just for an instant before I pressed it against his stomach where the worst of the cuts seemed to be. Tristan never moved. Didn't so much as flinch.

"Luna, listen to me."

My throat was thick with tears, but I managed to say, "I'm listening."

"Luca and I are about two hours away, but we're coming as fast as we can. Okay? Just hang in there, and try to stop the bleeding. If you can find the cell key, he has medical supplies in the bathroom off his bedroom."

"Okay." I pulled his shirt away and checked the wounds, then pressed it against his stomach again. My hand was shaking.

"Luna."

The sharp tone of his voice as he said my name snapped me out of my panic. "Yeah?"

"Stay with him."

"Where the fuck am I supposed to go, Enzo?" I snapped.

"Fuck. Sorry, I wasn't thinking. Just take care of him until we can get there."

Tristan's lips moved, but no sound came out.

My eyes on his face, I promised Enzo I would and dropped the phone on the floor. I heard him start to tell Luca what was going on right before he hung up. "Tristan?"

He didn't respond. I pulled the shirt away again, but there was so much blood smeared on his body I couldn't tell which cuts were the worst.

"I'll be right back." Jumping to my feet, I went into the bathroom and grabbed one of the soft, white towels he had in there for me, wetting one end.

When I came out, I accidentally kicked the drawing pad lying next to him with my bare foot. It slid to the side, revealing what was hiding beneath it.

Bending down, I picked it up. It was the picture of me and Logan. And there was blood on it.

I stared at it, not quite believing what I was seeing. He'd gone back to Gino's to get this picture for me. My eyes went back to Tristan, bleeding in the corner. Had Gino caught him? Had he done this?

"No..." I told him. "Oh, Tristan." The room blurred as my eyes filled with the tears I'd been trying so desperately to hold back. He'd gone back to Gino's, knowing it was a risk. Knowing how dangerous it was. But instead of killing him, Gino had done something far, far worse. "No, Tristan," I whispered.

Dropping the photo, I lowered myself to the floor beside him and, with the wet corner of the towel, started frantically wiping away the blood, thinking...what? That if I could only clean him up, it didn't really happen? Tears blurred my vision, and I couldn't see a damn thing.

"Get it off."

I sniffed and swiped at my eyes with the towel. Had he said something? "Tristan?" I searched his face, desperate to hear his voice one more time. His eyes were still staring straight ahead. Blood still seeped from the wounds on his torso, staining my hands as I pressed the towel over them.

"Get it off." His dead eyes found mine, and I almost cried out when I saw how lifeless they were. "Use the knife and get it off." His voice was raspy, like he'd been screaming.

What the hell had Gino done to him? "Get what off?"

He faded again, and his eyes slipped away from me. He was sitting right in front of me, and yet I'd never felt more alone.

"Tristan? Get what off? The blood?" With the knife? But that made no sense.

His upper lip lifted in disgust. "I can feel him. All over me. Get it off." His eyes found mine again, and this time my own flooded with tears when I saw the terror and pain inside of them.

He was showing me his pain.

My heart cracked inside my chest. I could barely manage to speak. "He's not here, Tristan. It's just me and you. We're in your cell. You're safe."

But his movements were frantic now as his hand felt around on the floor. "Where is it? Where the fuck is it?"

"Tristan, he's not here. You're okay."

"No. I can feel him. Touching me. Touching me everywhere." His voice broke as his chest rose and fell with frantic breaths. "He's touching me! Hurting me..." he trailed off.

My pulse pounded in my ears as I was suddenly filled with red-hot rage for the little boy he once was and the tortured man he'd become. Through gritted teeth, I said, "NO. He's not touching you."

"He is! I can fucking feel it." Pushing back into the wall, he struggled to his feet and his eyes landed on the knife where it had stopped near my blanket. He had it in his hand before I could stop him. His eyes were wild as he pressed the tip into the skin above the waistband of his pants, dragging it across his body and leaving a red line in its wake. He started to unfasten his pants.

"Tristan! Stop!" I lunged for the knife, but he held it up high where I couldn't reach it.

His eyes landed on my face, then fell to my breasts and down my body. His head tilted to the side and a mixture of anger and sorrow twisted his features. "His touch is on you, too."

My heart stopped. "No. No, it's not. I washed it off. We can wash it off you, too."

But he shook his head. "It doesn't work, Luna. I tried. Every day I try. You won't be able to get it off. Not now that you know what he is. What he did. It's all over you. I saw him through the window. I saw him touching you. Touching you everywhere."

I tried to swallow, but my throat was too dry. He was going to slice me open. Cut Gino's touch from my body. Possibly skin me alive. Oh, god. I should lock myself in the bathroom and wait for Enzo and Luca to show up. I should find the key and get the hell out of here. It had to be in his pocket. The right one. He always put it in the right pocket of his pants.

But I couldn't leave him. There'd be nothing left of him by the time they got here. Nothing but bloody strips of skin and raw muscle.

"He's not touching you, Tristan. *I'm* touching you." I laid my shaking hands on his chest, slippery with blood, ready to jump out of the way if that knife came down.

A horrific sound tore from his throat as he threw his head back.

"I'M touching you," I shouted over him. "It's me you feel. These are *my* hands. My touch. You don't belong to him. I don't belong to him, either. Look at me! Look!"

His head whipped forward as his jaw snapped shut and, if I didn't know better, I'd swear the devil himself was looking back at me. For a moment, I almost lost my nerve as his upper lip lifted and a snarl filled the air between us.

But he didn't jump away. And neither did I.

"It's me," I told him softly through my tears. "It's just me. Luna." Slowly, carefully now, I moved my hands, running them up over his shoulders and down his arms, feeling the texture of his scars and the raw wounds that would make new ones. "My hands. My touch," I repeated.

He stilled, pure fear shining from his eyes. "No. It's Gino," he whispered. "Gino's hands."

"NO," I insisted. "MY hands. Look. Look!" I continued to run my hands over his hard body.

After a moment, his chin dropped so he could see. His eyes traveled from my hands on his body, up my arms, and finally to my face. "Luna." My name was nothing but a deep rasp.

"Yes," I told him. "It's me. Just me. My touch on your skin." I grew bolder, touching him everywhere I could. He was stiff and still beneath my hands, but he didn't tell me to stop. "I love to touch you."

His eyes closed and his head fell back again, but this time, I saw a flash of relief in his expression. I could see the veins in his throat, his pulse racing. Rising onto my toes, I brushed my lips over them, then my tongue, taking his fear into me.

He moaned, and metal clattered against the floor as he dropped the knife. His hands found my hips and squeezed, and he lifted his head. Our eyes met, and his were filled with tears.

Stepping closer, I kissed a cut near his collarbone, then the one on the left side of his chest just above his nipple, tasting the salty copper of his blood. "My lips," I whispered against his skin.

"Luna." My name was both a prayer and a curse.

Still kissing him, I pulled off the long-sleeved shirt I wore, along with my soft yoga pants, and dropped them both on the floor. I wasn't wearing anything else. My bare breasts brushed his chest, my nipples hardening on contact. "My body," I told him. "It's just me."

"Just you," he repeated on a ragged breath. "My Luna."

"Yes. Just me."

A keening sound rose from his chest as his arms wrapped around my back and he pulled me tight against him. His head fell forward, his nose going into my hair. He inhaled deeply, his lips brushing the top of my head as he said, "My Luna."

"Yes," I told him.

His hand slid down my back to cup my ass, squeezing and holding me still as he rocked his hips against me. My breasts and stomach were wet with his blood, and his other hand was fisted in my hair. He tugged my head back until I exposed my throat to him. His lips were hot and frantic, his teeth sharp, as he kissed and sucked on my neck.

Oh, god. I was so lost in the feel of him.

CHAPTER 16

Tristan

Luna. Luna. Luna.

Her name was a mantra in my mind. It was Luna's hands touching me, burning my skin. Her scent filling my nose. Her taste on my tongue. Her soft breasts pressed against my chest. It stung, but I welcomed the pain. It kept me grounded in the now, not in my past, not in what happened to me tonight.

Her hands clung to my shoulders as I bent her back over my arm, my lips on her skin. She hesitated when I flinched.

"Don't stop," I pleaded. "Please, don't stop."

She dug her fingers into me, and my entire body shuddered. But she only pulled me closer. "It's just me," she said softly. "Just me."

I moaned, needing to touch her, too. We would purify each other of Gino's filthy touch. She was right. We didn't belong to him. We belonged to each other.

"You're not his," she repeated.

"No," I whispered against her throat. "I'm yours."

Luna stilled, but only for a moment before she wrapped her arms around me tight, pressing her body against mine. "Yesss," she hissed.

"And you're MINE," I growled.

Her hands shoved at my half-opened slacks, pushing them off my hips as I grabbed a handful of her hair and buried my face in the soft strands, inhaling the clean scent until I couldn't smell the leather of the couch or Gino's breath in my face.

When there was nothing else between us, I pulled her down to the blanket, rolling onto my back and settling her on top of me. I froze when her weight settled on me, trapping me beneath her, but she pressed herself against me, molding her body perfectly to mine. Skin on skin, I felt the slide of her thighs as she straddled me, and the wet heat of her pussy stroking my cock.

She reached between us, positioning me where I needed to be. I jerked my hips up as soon as the head of my cock felt her entrance, pushing inside of her, my eyes on her beautiful face as she cried out.

It was so much. Too much. And not enough. She was all around me now, touching me everywhere. "Luna," I groaned, a low sound of need and anguish as she began to move, our bodies slick with my blood.

"I'm here. You're safe with me." Her arms were on either side of my head and she tangled her fingers in my hair as she started to rock her hips.

Luna. My *bambolina*.

Fucking hell, I wanted her. I wanted her so badly.

I met her thrust for thrust, slamming into her with all the fear and hatred and need raging inside of me.

Wrapping my arms around her, I rolled until she was beneath me. And now her hands were on me again. They were fucking everywhere. Her legs wrapped around my hips, and the sensation was strange, and terrifying, as I waited for the pain that always came when someone touched me.

But even though I felt constrained, there was no pain, and I wanted more. Wanted to be closer. I wanted to bury myself so deep inside of her that there wouldn't be an inch of me she didn't touch. Overcome, I sank my teeth into the muscle between her neck and shoulder, holding her tight against me. Tears fell from my eyes to dampen her hair as my mind fought to stay there, with her.

"Let go, Tristan," she whispered, her arms wrapping around me as far as she could reach. "I've got you. It's okay. I've got you."

With a pained moan, I came undone.

I lost all control, my body taking over as I slid one knee up, forcing her legs to open wider so I could go even deeper, until there was only her. Only the feel of her skin, the smell of her hair, and the sound of her moans in my ears.

"Tristan!"

My name flew from her lips, and something cracked within me. I felt myself unravelling, and I cried out against her neck, my voice cracking from the intensity of my emotions. "Come with me," I ordered. "Come with me NOW."

As if she was only waiting for me, her body arched and jerked beneath me as my balls pulled up and my cock swelled to the point of bursting. My orgasm hit me, the intensity of it catching my breath and stopping my heart. Muscles shaking violently, I collapsed on top of her.

When I came back to myself, I heard her voice, singing some silly song breathlessly in my ear. Her hands stroked my scarred back, and her legs were still wrapped around me.

Lifting my head, I looked down into her blue eyes, shiny with tears, and kissed her until the passion between us flared once again.

I was forever altered.

I pulled away, panting, my heart still pounding in my chest, and traced the line of her jaw with my finger, the soft curve of her cheek. "Luna." I whispered her name in awe. Then I leaned down and kissed her again, this time with all the reverence I felt for her. I wanted to savor the moment, to imprint her taste and smell and feel on my memory. I had to be crushing her, but she kissed me back as though she wanted to do the same.

"You got my picture," she said as I kissed her jaw.

The photo. I'd almost forgotten about it. "Yes."

"You shouldn't have gone back there." As she talked, her hands stroked my back like it was the most natural thing in the world. Perhaps to her it was, but to me, the sensation was...unfamiliar. But surprisingly, it no longer burned my skin. As a matter of fact, I didn't want her to ever stop.

"I don't want to talk about this." No. The memory of tonight was already being stuffed into the lockbox of my mind where I kept all my childhood memories, only to be taken out and examined after enough time had passed that it will have seemed to have happened to someone else.

Shifting my weight off her, I laid on my side with my back to the bars and pulled her tight against me. It wasn't enough, so I tucked her underneath me a little more and held her as close as I could, throwing my leg over hers.

Her arm slid around my waist. Slowly.

I released a long, shaky breath and gradually, I relaxed as our breathing synced and our hearts slowed to an even, steady rhythm. She didn't try to talk anymore and, eventually, my eyes drifted shut. It was disconcerting at first, having her in here with me. But as I listened to her breathing even out and felt her body relax against me, a feeling of peace settled over me.

No one could get us here.

We were safe.

CHAPTER 17

Luna

"Luna."

I jolted awake, my whispered name like a scream in my ear in the silence. As I tried to slow my heartbeat, I looked around, getting my bearings. I was lying on my back on the soft blanket, and something heavy was lying half on top of me. My eyes flew to Tristan's face. He was lying over me, one muscular arm wrapped around my waist, his heavy thigh trapping both of mine, and his head on my chest. His breathing was even and deep. We were both naked, but for once, I wasn't cold.

My chest ached to find him like this, and I wondered how he'd react when he woke up. Would he still be okay with me touching him? Or would he retreat back inside his walls?

Tilting my head up, I found Enzo sitting on his haunches outside the cell near our heads, with his elbows resting on his knees. His face was turned away, giving us as much privacy as he could. "Enzo?" My voice was rusty, and I cleared my throat.

"Are you okay?" he asked. "Is Tristan okay?"

"I think so," I told him. Reaching for the blanket, I pulled one corner over my hips, covering as much as I could.

Tristan stirred in my arms. I rubbed his back with my free hand, and he moaned softly, the muscles beneath my palm twitching, but he didn't wake.

I glanced up in time to catch Enzo watching me comfort him before he quickly looked away again. With his sunglasses on, I couldn't read his expression, but I could well imagine what he was thinking.

"How are you touching him?" His voice was filled with awe. "No one has touched him since he was a child. At least not without earning a violent reaction."

"Can we talk about this later?"

Immediately, he stood. "Of course. Forgive me. I'll let you get dressed and wait in the kitchen. The key to the cell is in the door. I found it on the floor. I was going to come in, but I didn't want to set him off again."

"Thank you."

Once Enzo left the bedroom, I tried to slip out from beneath Tristan without waking him. But he was heavy, and I couldn't get out from underneath him without jostling him awake.

"Where are you going?" he growled sleepily.

I released a breath when all he did was tighten his hold on me. "Enzo is here."

He lifted his head. His eyes fell to my face, studying my features before he looked behind him. I couldn't tell what he was thinking.

"Where is he?"

"He's waiting in the kitchen."

His eyes snapped back to me. "Was he in here?"

"Yes."

"Did he see you like this?"

A chill slithered down my spine at this tone. "I called him when...earlier. He just wanted to make sure we were both okay."

A heartbeat passed. Then another. "And are you?"

I thought I heard the slightest thread of concern. "Yes." I gave him a small smile.

Instead of returning it, he brushed his lips against mine. It was then that I realized I'd never seen him smile. Ever.

Rolling off me, he sat up, keeping one hand on my leg. The scars on his back were longer than the ones on his front. Thicker. Like marks I'd seen on old photographs of people who were whipped.

"Do you remember what happened tonight? With us?" I clarified.

He glanced over his shoulder at me. His hair was messed up from my fingers, but he was nonetheless still imposing. "Yes." He turned his face away, dropping his chin and tilting his head side to side to stretch the muscles in his neck.

I sat up. There was dried blood all over my chest and stomach. Some had even smeared on my hips and the tops of my thighs. I looked like a horror movie.

"Do I disgust you, Luna?"

The question was so quiet I almost didn't hear him. "No," I told him honestly. He didn't disgust me, physically or otherwise. He scared me sometimes, but not as much anymore. Cautiously, I placed my hand on his back. He stiffened, but only slightly this time, before he relaxed again. I traced one of his scars with my fingertip.

"I don't want your pity."

I stared at his handsome profile. "There's a difference between pity and commiseration. Or comfort." I did feel sorry for him, and there was nothing wrong with that. It meant I was a compassionate human being, not that he was weak. If anything, the trials he'd gone through—and still went through—only made him stronger in my eyes. Most people, me included, wouldn't have survived the horrors he had.

But I didn't say any of that. Not now. One day, maybe.

I was startled to think we'd have a "one day" sometime in the future. The notion that I envisioned there still being an "us" months or years from now caught me off guard. When had I started thinking of him as anything other than my stalker?

"What is it?"

"Hmm?" I blinked away the thought. "Oh, nothing. Just thinking I need a shower."

He made a sound of agreement and rose to his feet, drawing me up with him. Finding his pants, he pulled them on as I wrapped the blanket around myself. "The key is in the door," I told him when I saw him looking around. His chest and stomach looked like he'd been in a knife fight, which, I suppose, in a way he had. It had to hurt, but he didn't seem affected at all. He still moved with the same smooth grace he always had.

I stayed where I was as he gathered up his shirt and opened the cell door. His eyes had flickered over the knife on the floor, but he'd left it where it was. "Come on," he told me. "Get some clothes. We'll move your things later."

Move my things? Did that mean he was letting me out of this fucking cell for good? Why? I wanted to ask him what he meant by that. Was he letting me go? But...

I didn't want to leave.

That truth shook me so much I couldn't bring myself to ask him anything. I was afraid to. Afraid I wouldn't like his answers.

We showered in his bathroom. He washed my long hair and scrubbed his blood from my body in silence. Then he washed every inch of me. I didn't push him to talk, or to accept more of my touch. It was enough that he didn't have me handcuffed.

I couldn't take my eyes from him as he washed himself, the water running in rivulets through his scars. Beneath them, his body, though not bulky, was hard and muscular and perfectly formed. As my gaze traveled down his abs to the "V" at his hips and the tuft of dark, curly hair there, his cock thickened.

"Stop looking at me like that, or Enzo will be waiting a very long time."

I smiled. Would that be a bad thing? When I looked up, he was watching me with a strange expression on his face.

"You should let me bandage those," I told him as he rinsed his hair, indicating the self-mutilations on his chest and stomach. "Doesn't it hurt?" A few of the cuts had started bleeding again with the water and his movements.

He didn't even glance down. "Yes."

"Then you should let me help you."

Turning off the water, he opened the shower door and grabbed a towel from the rack, wrapping it around me after drying my hair and body. "You can do it while I talk to Enzo," he finally told me.

I stepped out while he dried himself and went into the bedroom to get dressed. By the time he came out, I was sitting on the bed, running a comb through my wet hair.

"We need to talk, Luna." Pulling on some clean lounge pants, he left his chest bare and went back into the bathroom to get his first aid supplies. I was waiting for him when he came out. "But not tonight. Tomorrow," he said. "Tomorrow, we'll talk."

I stared up at him, but then I nodded. "Okay. I can wait until tomorrow."

Wrapping his hand around my throat, he forced my head up so I was looking at him. My heart raced as I stared up at him. "What is it?" I asked him.

He looked like he was about to say something, but then he just ran his thumb along my jaw as his eyes roamed over my face. "Tomorrow."

Taking my hand, he led me out to see Enzo, and to my surprise, Luca was there, too. A bottle of whiskey sat on the table, and they both had empty glasses in front of them. Luca's eyes ran over me quickly before he gave me a nod hello.

"Jesus Christ, Tristan," Luca said when he saw him. "What the hell happened?"

Tristan leaned back against the counter, his hands gripping the edge while I dug through the stuff he'd brought out. I found some gauze, peroxide, butterfly bandages, and Vaseline. While he talked to his boss and Enzo, I cleaned and bandaged the worst of his wounds. He didn't seem to notice when I poured peroxide into the cuts, catching it on the gauze. Didn't even flinch when I closed a few with butterfly bandages. But I saw his knuckles whiten when Gino's name was mentioned.

"Why did you go back there?" Luca asked him.

"I thought I'd take a look around while he wasn't there, see if I could find anything. And I'd forgotten something important for Luna. But it was all a ruse. He was waiting for me." He paused. "It was my fault. I let my guard down and one of his men snuck up on me. I didn't have time to react before the chemicals took effect." He stopped, glancing at me before giving his attention back to Luca.

I had the feeling he didn't want to say too much with me in the room. "I'm just gonna put this stuff away," I told him quietly. "I'll wait for you in the bedroom."

His hand struck out fast as a snake and wrapped around my wrist. My eyes flew to his, expecting to see the same cold stare. But instead, I saw a flash of fear in his dark eyes. "No. Stay."

I glanced over at Luca and Enzo, who were watching this interaction with interest. When neither of them objected, I leaned against the counter beside him.

"Did you find anything of interest?" Luca asked after a moment.

"No," Tristan told him. "I didn't have a chance. I never made it out of Luna's room."

To their credit, neither Luca nor Enzo took his answer as anything more than a normal report, and didn't press him for more.

"Alright," Luca told him. "I'd like to see you and Enzo in my office tomorrow, T. If you feel up to it."

"I'm fine," he told him. "I'll be there in the morning."

I watched Luca and Enzo leave, feeling a mixture of relief and apprehension now that Tristan and I were alone again.

As soon as the door closed behind them, Tristan turned to me. His dark eyes were unreadable as they searched my face. "Are you hungry?"

I almost said no, but then I nodded. Normal things. That's what he needed. Normal things always made me feel better when I got too in my head. And I *was* hungry. "Yeah, I'm starving."

"Why don't you go move your things into my room while I make something."

"Your room?" I couldn't keep the surprise in my voice.

He studied my face. "Yes. I want you to stay with me now."

For how long? I wanted to ask. *And what about Gino?* Was he dead? Is that why he was letting me out? But I assumed he would've told Luca if that was the case, unless he didn't want me to know for some reason. I set my questions aside for now. I was getting out of that fucking cell and that worked for me.

It didn't take long for me to transfer my meager belongings into his bedroom. I left my clothes in the bag they were in, and set my bathroom supplies beside it, not sure how comfortable I should make myself.

When I finished, I went back to the kitchen. Tristan was standing over the stove, stirring something in a deep frying pan. I hovered in the doorway, unsure if I should join him or give him space.

"I just threw together some pasta," he said without looking away from what he was doing.

"Pasta's great," I told him. "Thank you."

I watched him cook, struck by what a dichotomy he was—a man who killed without conscience, yet took pleasure in such a simple domestic task.

Once the food was ready, he set a plate down in front of me at the table and took the seat across from mine. Other than my groans of pleasure every time I put a bite in my mouth, we ate in silence.

When we finished, I found Tristan's eyes on me, and I gave him a questioning look.

"Would you sit for me one day soon?"

"Sit for you?"

"I'd like to draw you. Properly," he added. "Not from memory."

I frowned at him. "The pictures in the room. You drew them from memory?" The idea was crazy to me. I could barely draw an apple.

"Yes. But they're not right."

They looked pretty damn good to me. "Oh. Uh, sure." I guess that answered the question of whether or not he planned for me to stay. Looked like I'd be here for a while, at least.

"Thank you."

A smile teased the corners of my mouth. "You're welcome."

I picked up our plates, leaving them in the sink when he told me to, and we made our way back to the bedroom. He eyed my things, all together in the corner, but said nothing as I left him in the bedroom to get ready for bed.

I was tucked into my side when he came out and turned off the light. I heard the rustle of his lounge pants hitting the floor, and then felt the dip of the mattress.

Unlike the last time I was in his bed, he didn't keep his distance. Instead, he climbed beneath the covers, found me in the darkness, and pulled me close to him. When he found me still clothed, he silently stripped me bare again.

I didn't protest as he tucked me beneath him, covering as much of my body as he could with his until we were skin to skin everywhere he could reach. When my arms came around him, he released a heavy, shuddering sigh. "Is this okay?" I asked him. "Is it too much?"

"Yes," he whispered. "And not enough." After a long pause, he asked quietly, "Why didn't you run, Luna?"

I knew he was talking about when Enzo left the key in the cell. "I don't know," I told him honestly.

"He would've let you go."

After a pause, I confessed, "I didn't want to leave you." He always gave me the truth, as far as I knew. And he deserved the same from me.

He was quiet for a bit. "Because of Gino?" There wasn't an ounce of emotion in his voice when he said his name.

A sure sign, I was learning, that it was something that disturbed him a lot.

"No. I wanted to stay with you."

His fingers dug into my hip. "Why?"

I started to tell him it was because I wanted to make sure he was okay, but that wasn't the complete truth. I stayed because...I cared. "Because I wanted to be with you. And I was worried."

Slowly, his fingers loosened their hold on me. "If you ran, I would've come for you." He pressed his lips to the top of my head. "I'll always come for you, Luna."

He drew back enough to meet my eyes. Even in the dark, the intensity in his gaze made me shiver. I knew he meant what he said, but it didn't frighten me. Instead, a warm feeling surged inside of me. Other than my brother, no one had ever cared enough about me to care if I was there or not. Not my foster parents. Not the men I danced for— and fucked. They were all just using me, just like I used them.

But I wasn't lying when I'd told him I cared. My feelings for this dangerous man were complicated, but they were there, no matter how hard I tried to fight them.

The realization was both thrilling and terrifying.

I lifted my hand to his cheek, brushing my thumb over his sculpted cheekbone. His eyes fluttered shut at my touch.

"What are you doing to me, Luna?" he murmured.

Before I could respond, he kissed me.

CHAPTER 18

Luna

When I woke up, Tristan was gone. I found a note on the counter ordering me not to leave the house or unlock the door for anyone but him, and that there was a covered plate in the microwave for me. I smiled. If I didn't know better, I'd think he was trying to fatten me up.

I had some coffee and ate the waffle breakfast he'd left me, then took another shower and brushed my teeth again. When I was done, I eyed my bag of clothes, and then the dresser beside it. Opening one of the drawers, I found boxer briefs and socks, all in black. The next drawer had T-shirts and long-sleeved shirts, like the one he'd had on the other night. The colors of both were all dark and muted. Nothing bright. Nothing colorful.

Beneath his shirts I found a drawer with three pairs of lounge pants. The bottom drawer held a few pairs of black tactical pants and long-sleeved black shirts. A shiver ran down my spine when I remembered these were the clothes he'd had on when he snuck into my room.

All the drawers on the right side were empty.

Chewing my thumbnail, I wandered over to his closet and found a good number of expensive black suit jackets hanging neatly. Beneath them was another rod that held his slacks neatly folded over hangers. On the other side, there was a row of black dress shirts, and two white shirts. On the floor, there was a pair of boots and a pair of white running shoes. I assumed he was wearing his dress shoes. A tie rack hung on the wall at the back with a few black ties. I let one slide between my fingers, feeling the silky texture. Taking a deep breath, I inhaled his scent. The muscles low in my belly clenched with need.

In the end, I left my clothes in the bag, but I did leave my shampoo and conditioner in the shower, along with the body wash I liked. My other bathroom items I arranged on the counter alongside his. Stepping back, I looked at our things sitting there together and wondered when exactly I'd stopped thinking of escaping.

I'll always come for you, Luna.

Trying not to overthink things, I unplugged my cell and put it in the pocket of my jeans so I could text or call

Logan when his classes were out, then wandered through the rest of the house. There were only two areas I hadn't seen—a living area off the kitchen and his office.

Like the rest of the house, the living room was neat and clean, the walls unadorned. There was a black leather love seat and a matching chair facing a small fireplace that looked like it had never been used. A simple gray area rug covered the floor. No television. But there were some books on a bookshelf near the windows. Curious, I went over to check them out, running my fingers over the spines as I read the titles. I found a wide array of subjects. Everything from architecture and war to near death experiences. I noticed it was all nonfiction. Not a fantasy or mystery in sight.

Moving on, I went across the hall to his office. I hesitated before I went in. But then I figured if he'd wanted me to stay out, he would've at least shut the door and not left it wide open in invitation, so I went in.

His office was small. Everything neat and in its place. Against the wall to my right was a black leather loveseat and a glass coffee table. Directly in front of me was a small black desk faced so his back would be to the wall when he sat at it. On the desk was a computer monitor, mouse, and keyboard. The chair was a luxurious black leather, similar to the couch. The wall behind it was bare except for a small corner window to the right. On my left was a matching bookshelf near the desk, taller than the one in the living room, and on the wall beside it was a generic painting of the Austin skyline. The same painting you could find hanging in at least half of the restaurants in the area.

It was strange to me that he had that painting in particular. From what I knew of Tristan, he wasn't a man who bought a painting just to fill a space on the wall. As a matter of fact, his entire home was very...generic. The outside was stone. The inside had gray walls and laminate ash wood flooring. All the furniture was black, even the ceiling fans. The kitchen and bathrooms had dark gray cabinets and white counters. There was no other decor, unless you counted the drawings of me, which were obviously very personal and still creeped me out just a little.

So, why this particular painting?

Walking over to it, I studied it for a minute, trying to find some reason Tristan would have this hanging in his office. When I saw nothing of interest, I pulled on the bottom right corner a little.

To my surprise, the entire right side of the painting swung out from the wall about an inch.

What the hell?

I tried to see what was behind it, but the window didn't let in much light. I carefully tugged a little harder, half expecting the entire thing to fall to the floor. But it didn't. It swung out more. Enough that I could see the small safe behind it.

My conscience spoke up then, telling me to put the painting back and leave it alone. It was none of my business what was in that safe. Besides, I was absolutely positive it would be locked.

I tried the handle beside the keypad, and, to my surprise, it opened easily.

Too curious to turn back now, I lifted onto my toes and peered inside. A stack of photos rested on top of a pile of papers. Leaving the papers, I pulled out the pictures and looked through a few of them.

At first, I didn't know what I was looking at. They appeared to be random photos of different men. Some wore suits and/or looked to be mafia. Others just looked like random guys of all different ages.

"Weird," I said to the empty room. I was putting the photos back when I saw one that I'd missed. Thinking it came from the bottom of the pile, I pulled it out and glanced at the people in it. My heart stopped in my chest, and for a moment, I couldn't breathe.

I was looking at an image of my mother and me. It had been taken a few weeks before she died.

Why would Tristan have this picture?

I glanced at the other photos, then back at the one of my mom, my mind trying to make the connection. I was missing something obvious.

Wait. This guy. I knew this guy. He used to come to the poker games at the club. He wasn't much of a player, but he liked to throw his money around. And then one week he just stopped showing up. The funny thing was, no one mentioned it. His name was never tossed around. No one wondered where he was or why he didn't show up anymore.

I looked at his picture again, then a few others. As I went back to the photo of me and my mom, an idea started to form, but I shook my head before it could even become coherent. No. That couldn't be right.

But why else would he have all these photos? Why would my mother be one of them?

My *dead* mother.

The realization I was trying so hard to deny sliced through me, more painful than any cut a knife would make.

"No," I whispered, shaking my head. "No," I said, louder. Was I really that stupid? That naive?

Tears filled my eyes as the photos slipped from my hands and fell to the floor. I stared down at them, internally screaming that I was wrong, and knowing I wasn't.

My phone vibrated in my pocket. In somewhat of a daze, I pulled it out and looked down at the screen, reading the text there. The photos were forgotten as terror flooded through me, freezing my feet to the floor.

CHAPTER 19

Tristan

When I walked into Luca's office the next morning, he was alone. "Where's Enzo?"

"On his way. I wanted to talk to you alone first."

"About what?"

Leaning back in his desk chair, he leveled a steady stare my way. "Are you all right, Tristan? Is there anything I can do?"

My answer was immediate. "You can let me kill him."

"I'd like to know what happened."

I pressed my lips together. I didn't want to talk about it.

Luca came to stand in front of me, not too close. "Talk to me, T."

I lifted my chin. "It doesn't matter what happened. I'm still here."

"It does to me. Did he...hurt you?"

I glanced toward the window, noticing the sun was coming out. "In what way?"

"I think you know what I'm asking."

My eyes flew to his, my breath freezing in my lungs. And for a moment, I couldn't speak. "Spell it out for me, Luca."

His gray eyes softened. "I know what happened between you and Gino when you were younger. So does Enzo. You don't have to hide anything from us."

My lip curled, baring my teeth. "It wasn't your business," I spit out. My past was just that. MINE. There was a reason I'd never told the two people closest to me what happened during the years his father and his cronies were "molding" me.

Because I didn't want them to *fucking* know.

"What did he do to you yesterday?"

I stared at him, but said nothing.

He changed tactics. "How many men did it take to restrain you?"

"Four," I answered. "And some chains."

"Jesus." But there was a glimmer of pride in his eyes.

"I got away before..." I trailed off, unable to form the words. "I took some hits. That's all."

"But he was going to hurt you." It wasn't a question.

After a moment, I turned my face away. "Yes," I said quietly.

He was quiet for a long time. "How many of them did you kill?"

"All of them. I think." I frowned. "Except Gino. When it was over, he was gone."

Luca nodded. "I sent Milo to his house. And I've got men trying to find him."

"Let me find the *bastardo*."

"I don't know if that's a good idea, my friend."

I'd always followed Luca's orders without question. It never mattered to me. But this time...this time, it fucking mattered. "I think it's an excellent idea."

There was a knock on the doorframe and Enzo walked in. He greeted Luca before turning to me. "You doing okay, T?"

My eyes never left my boss. "I'm good."

Luca picked up the conversation where he'd left off. "As soon as we find Gino, I'll bring him in here and we'll deal with him. Together."

I didn't want them with me when I found Gino. As a capo who'd been in the family his entire life, Luca would insist he have an honorable death. He'd want to handle Gino's crimes the right way, with the family behind him.

I didn't want him to have an honorable death. I wanted to give him the death he deserved. The death he was owed after what he did to me. After what he made me.

And what he'd done to his own daughter. The daughter he'd wanted nothing to do with until she was all grown up. Until, in his sick mind, she became her mother.

A buzzing noise started up in my head, so loud I could barely hear what anyone was saying, but I didn't bother arguing with Luca. There was no point. He was the boss, and I was his soldier. I'd follow his orders, even if I didn't agree with them.

Until it suited me to do otherwise.

I had a hard time holding still while he filled me and Enzo in on his plan to find Gino. He'd already called a meeting with the rest of the capos in the area so he could fill them in on his suspicions that Gino was, indeed, a traitor to *La Cosa Nostra*. He would also tell them about his recent behavior with Luna.

"I want to bring her into the meeting."

"No," I growled. "That's not happening. She hasn't had time to deal with what he did to her." She was in denial. I was very familiar with that stage of processing a traumatic experience, so I recognized it easily. One day soon, it would hit her, and she would break. And it didn't need to be in a room full of old Italian men.

"It will have more impact if she tells them herself," Enzo agreed.

"No," I repeated.

Luca sighed. "Perhaps we should ask Luna if she'd be willing to do it."

I clenched my jaw until it ached, the tension radiating through my face. He was right. We should ask her. But that didn't mean I was going to allow it. I slowly nodded in agreement. "We can ask her, but I won't promise anything more."

"Good," Luca said, seemingly satisfied with my concession. "Finding Gino is my top priority, Tristan. I want you to know that. And I'll be sure to keep you fully updated on any developments."

"Thank you," I told him sincerely.

He wrapped up the rest of the meeting shortly after, dismissing me for the remainder of the day. The only thing that kept me from insisting I could work was that it gave me more uninterrupted time with Luna. Plus, I wasn't at all comfortable leaving her roaming freely about the house while her father was still missing and a potential threat. Although I wouldn't hesitate to lock her back in the cell again if I couldn't remain close by, it would be good for us if I didn't have to today.

I couldn't head home just yet, though. I was too worked up. And I wanted to hit something. Plus, I needed some time to gather my thoughts before I saw Luna again. We had the rest of the day to talk, among other things, and I didn't want my head to be all fucked up when we did.

Already, I craved her touch. After so long alone, I was starved for it. I wanted to hold her like I did last night, skin to skin. Needed to be inside of her so deep there was nothing else but Luna. No one else but me and my *bambolina*. Safe. We were safe as long as we were together.

"I'm going to head to the gym and work out for a while," I told them both.

"Are you sure that's a good idea?" Luca asked. "You're still healing, Tristan."

Whether he was referring to my physical or mental wounds, I didn't know. But the only thing that would make me feel better right now was inflicting pain. And since my preferred victim was out there hiding somewhere like the pussy he really was, and I didn't want to take this out on my friends, it would have to be the punching bag.

"I'll be fine." Without another word, I left Luca's office and took the hall down to the large room at the end. The expansive space housed a full gym, including a sparring

ring. Changing into the workout clothes I kept there, I bypassed the weights and treadmill and went straight to the heavy bag.

Not bothering with tape or gloves, I started throwing punches, alternating between my left and right, and throwing kicks in between. I just needed to hit something. Hard.

The rhythmic smack of my fists against the bag echoed through the empty room. Right, left, right. Right, left, right. Kick. I sank into the mindless repetition, losing myself in the burn of my muscles. My knuckles split, blood smearing the bag with each punch. More of it seeped through my shirt where my wounds had reopened. I didn't stop, didn't even feel it. I just kept hitting until the buzzing in my head went away.

Footsteps echoed through the room, and I paused mid-punch, glancing over my shoulder to see who it was. Enzo walked toward me, hands in the front pockets of his dress slacks. I turned back to the bag and threw another combination. Unless he was going to volunteer to fight me, I wasn't interested.

"How're you holding up?" he asked.

I didn't answer, just kept punching. Taking my cue, Enzo came over and held the bag steady for me. He didn't ask me any more questions as I continued my workout, hitting the bag with focused intensity. After twenty more minutes, I finally stepped back, chest heaving. I wiped the sweat from my brow with the back of my hand.

"Better?" Enzo asked.

I nodded, still catching my breath.

Through his dark glasses, I felt the intensity of his stare. "Luca wants to handle this his way."

My jaw clenched. "I know."

"But you don't agree."

I met his gaze. "Gino needs to suffer. Luca won't make him suffer."

Enzo was quiet for a moment. "If you go after Gino yourself, it could cause more problems within the family. You know that."

"Yes. I know." I looked down and flexed my bloody, battered hands.

He took off his glasses and rubbed the bridge of his nose. "But you're still going to do it."

Lifting my chin, I met his eyes. "Yes."

I held his stare without flinching as Enzo searched my face. Then he nodded slowly. "Okay." He understood me. If I was going to war with Gino over this, he'd stand with me. But I wouldn't ask him to get involved.

"If you need me, T, just call me. For anything. You know that."

"I do."

With a nod, he left me to it.

I turned back to the heavy bag and unleashed another barrage of punches, letting the pain that lanced through my hands ground me.

When I was so exhausted my muscles trembled and my fists slid off the bag, I showered, washing away the blood, and wrapped my knuckles with gauze before checking the cuts on my torso and getting dressed.

As I headed back to the house, my hands throbbed, but the pain helped quiet my mind, except for one thought...

I was going to kill Gino. No matter what it took.

The front door was unlocked when I got back to the house. I froze with my hand on the knob, then I let go and backed up a few steps, looking around. Nothing was out of place as far as I could tell.

Removing my gun from its holster, I stood to the side and pushed the door open. When no bullets came flying at me, I peeked around the corner into the kitchen. It was empty.

I kicked off my dress shoes and left them outside. Silently, I entered the house, pistol at the ready. The living room was empty, as was my office. I kept going all the way back to the spare bedroom. The cell and its adjoining bathroom were empty.

My bedroom was next, but a quick sweep showed me it was also empty. The bed was made, and Luna's things were still there. I paused when I saw her girly items on the bathroom counter by mine, and there was a strange flutter in my stomach.

Lowering my gun but keeping it in my hand, I left my room to go check outside. It was chilly, but the sun was out. Perhaps she went for a walk on the grounds, despite the fact I told her to stay in the house.

"Luna!" I called her name over and over as I searched, but she was nowhere outside. With a shaking hand, I pulled out my cell phone and called Luca's house. No one had seen her.

My phone slipped from my fingers and fell to the wet ground.

Luna was gone.

END OF BOOK 2.

ABOUT THE AUTHOR

Hi! My name is Angel Rayne and I write dark, delicious romance with antiheroes who would burn down the world to save the woman they love. I never understood why the villains never win the girl, and so I decided to write them their own love stories where they do.

Here are a few other odds and ends about me...

-Music inspires my stories and I make playlists for every book.

-I am not a fast writer. My stories take time to write. They need to brew in my head. To have book releases close together I have to write ahead. But I would much rather take the time the stories need to be the best they can be than try to rush them out. Trust me on this one.

-I love the rain, and I'm happiest when I'm sitting in a coffee shop with my laptop as it storms outside.

-I prefer to go watch movies alone, with one of those fancy coffees hidden in my purse. (Yes, I really do this.)

-My husband calls me his "little bird" because anything that sparkles catches my eye.

-I will never have enough soft blankets. Ever.

-I love ALL THE DRAMA...but only in books.

-I will forever re-watch The Phantom of the Opera with the hope that by some miracle, this time Christine will choose the right guy.

Thank you for reading my stories, and I always love to hear from you! You can reach me at: angel@angelrayne.com